"We can't find Penn!"

"Don't—" an usher burst into sight, gasping "—don't give the cue yet. We can't find Penn anywhere."

Kaitlyn could actually feel the blood draining from her face. "Has he been here at all?"

Another usher appeared in the stairwell. "Oh, yes. He *was* here."

He can't possibly stand me up at the church, Kaitlyn told herself. "He didn't happen to mention Botswana or the Sahara Desert or Tahiti, did he?"

"He didn't say anything." The usher shrugged helplessly. "He was just gone all of a sudden."

A third usher rushed in. "Is he here?"

Kaitlyn put her head in her hands. "I'm never going through this again."

"I should hope not." Penn's calm voice came from behind her. "Only one wedding to a customer!"

Dear Reader,

One of my very earliest memories is of a wedding. It was night—or at least it seemed later than I'd ever been allowed to stay up before—and the church was hushed and candlelit. Then the bride appeared, in the most luscious Southern-belle dress I'd ever seen, and as she came down the aisle on her father's arm, she looked at a four-year-old girl standing on the church pew and hanging over the end . . . and she smiled at me.

I've been in love with weddings ever since.

On the June day when I was married, the church was filled with candles, a violinist played Bach and as we passed under an archway of swords, the organ thundered a recessional and then switched to ragtime so everyone would be in the right mood for the reception. Everything was perfect elegance.

At least, it should have been. But it was so hot in the church that the candles didn't just drip, they melted down and bent over. The usher who was supposed to give the cue for the whole proceedings forgot, leaving a breathless hush when everyone must have wondered if the wedding was going to be canceled. My beloved insisted on taking photographs during his own wedding ceremony.

Fortunately for me, my romantic turn of mind has always been spiced by an appreciation of the ridiculous—and seventeen years later, the funny memories are the fondest ones of all.

Sincerely,

Leigh Michaels

THE BEST-MADE PLANS

Leigh Michaels

Harlequin Books

TORONTO • NEW YORK • LONDON
AMSTERDAM • PARIS • SYDNEY • HAMBURG
STOCKHOLM • ATHENS • TOKYO • MILAN
MADRID • WARSAW • BUDAPEST • AUCKLAND

ISBN 0-373-03214-5

Harlequin Romance first edition August 1992

THE BEST-MADE PLANS

CHAPTER ONE

THE CHURCH was not silent. It was filled with tiny noises—
the soft ripple of the organ playing a popular love song,
the low murmurs of the congregation, the occasional
cough and the rustle of Sunday-best clothes as a last, late-
arriving guest was seated. Still, underneath the surface
sounds, the church held an expectant hush that Kaitlyn
Ross had learned to recognize. It used to bother her; it had
seemed almost as if the guests were hopeful that something scandalous would happen. Now she knew that it was
always like this in the last few moments before the bride
came down the aisle. It was nothing to fret about.

She stepped quietly into a small nook near the altar,
where almost no one could see her, for a final quick survey to make sure everything was in place. She didn't intend to be noticed, of course; that was why, on days like
this, she dressed so sedately—today, it was a very plain
coffee-brown dress and only the simplest of jewelry—and
moved so discreetly along the side aisles and through the
back corridors, checking—always checking.

From this perfect vantage point, her eyes could rove over
every inch of St. Matthew's, noting that each satin ribbon
was neatly in place, each candle straight and burning
freely, each flower nodding proudly on the altar. Moss
green and peach this time—and a lovely combination it
had turned out to be. She was so glad she had steered Angela—and, what had been even more difficult, Angela's

mother—away from the heavy midnight blue they had originally talked of. Midnight blue on a hot June evening, for heaven's sake!

With her survey of the church completed, Kaitlyn peeked into the clergyman's chambers to be certain the groom hadn't fled in panic, and then made her way unobtrusively down the side aisle with only a silent nod and a smile to a friend here and a client there. Halfway back on the bride's side, she noticed her mother; Audrey Ross caught her daughter's eye and gave her a subtle thumbs-up sign.

Encouragement? Kaitlyn blinked in surprise. This wedding was going to be a snap; what could go wrong at this stage? Still, it was sweet of Audrey to offer that sign of confidence, whether it was needed or not.

She was nearly to the back of the church before she saw him.

He was sitting by himself, in an almost-hidden corner, as if he had slipped in unannounced at the last moment. But he hadn't been unseen; that was obvious, for now Kaitlyn knew why her mother had issued that small gesture of support. Audrey had spotted him, and she was reassuring her daughter. Reassuring her, and perhaps pleading innocence, as well—disavowing any previous knowledge that Penn would be here today.

Not that it matters, Kaitlyn told herself. So what if Penn came home for his cousin Angela's wedding? There was nothing in his presence to upset Kaitlyn, after all these years.

Penn Caldwell, she mused. Charming, funny, fascinating Penn Caldwell. And also, she reminded herself, stubborn, determined, egotistical Penn Caldwell, never the sort to settle down to one place—or to one woman.

So Penn was home, after ten years of roaming the world.

The funny thing was, Kaitlyn thought, that a casual observer would have assumed the man was a lawyer, or a doctor, or the mechanical engineer his father had wanted him to be. He looked solid and reliable and competent, with his perfectly tailored pale gray suit and his expertly cut black hair. Only the rich tan of his skin, which spoke of hours in the sun, didn't quite fit with that professional image.

What he certainly did not look like was a journeyman laborer, or a Peace Corps volunteer, or a part-time taxi driver, or an assistant dishwasher, or a surfing instructor—but he had been all of those incongruous things and more over the years. Not that he had ever sent so much as a postcard to Kaitlyn, but in a town the size of Springhill, a good story always got around. And when the story concerned Penn Caldwell—the promising young man who had taken such a puzzling turn after the tragedy that had struck his family—it got around very quickly indeed.

Penn looked up as she approached, and Kaitlyn found herself staring straight into his cool dark gray eyes, her own green ones widening just a bit, despite herself, at the impact of that gaze. With an effort, she let her gaze slide across his, and she walked on, a little faster, eager to reach the back of the church and get this wedding under way.

But at the end of the pew where he sat, her foot came down wrong on the flagstone floor, and the high heel of her sandal squealed a protest as it slid sideways over the slick stone. Half the congregation's members craned their necks expectantly at the sound.

Penn's arm shot out in front of her, and Kaitlyn clutched it until she regained her balance. "Thank you," she muttered. She pulled away as quickly as she could and tried to suppress the embarrassed color in her cheeks as she hurried on down the aisle.

Damn St. Matthew's council, she thought irritably. The uneven stones were dangerous to start with, but instead of doing something helpful, the church authorities just kept adding coats of wax.

The organist began to play another love song, and outside the sanctuary doors Angela's mother stopped pacing and said, "Is that my cue?" She looked distractedly from the doors to the tiny anteroom where the bride waited, as if she couldn't make up her mind which direction to go.

Kaitlyn patted her arm. "It will be fine, Mrs. March," she told the woman, and sent her into the church on the arm of one of the ushers before she could do more than cast another longing look toward her daughter.

Honestly, Kaitlyn thought. If people didn't have someone to manage them on occasions like this, nothing would ever get done! What had kept things moving before there were wedding consultants to do the organizing?

She glanced into the anteroom, where the photographer was setting up a last pose of Angela with her bridesmaids and a tiny flower girl, who looked ready to cry.

That's all we need, Kaitlyn thought. "It's time, girls. Better get into position inside the sanctuary, Jill."

The photographer, a young woman in a dark gray dress that made no attempt to conceal the fact that she was very pregnant, snapped the final shot and gathered up her equipment. "Ready when you are."

Kaitlyn marshaled the bridesmaids into line, signaled the organist, and counted the measure so each of the girls got off at the right moment, on the right foot—a minor miracle in itself, after the way things had looked at rehearsal. She just hoped none of them stepped off the white carpet runner and onto that uncertain flagstone floor, for Penn might not be there to hold on to.

The muscles of his arm had been like steel cables, she thought. Well, there was one story going the rounds about Penn that she would never doubt again; he'd certainly been doing some sort of physical labor, somewhere, to build up that kind of strength.

Under cover of the last few bars of the wedding march, Kaitlyn slipped up the side aisle again and into the spot beside her mother.

"Dearly beloved," the clergyman began. "We are gathered—"

Audrey muttered, "Penn's here."

"I saw him."

"You didn't mention that he was coming."

"I didn't know he was. He didn't have the good manners even to answer the invitation." Kaitlyn buried herself in the wedding program, pretending fascination as if she'd never seen it before.

The gesture obviously didn't fool her mother, but Audrey sighed and fanned herself with her own program and turned her attention back to the ceremony.

As if he would have let me know, Kaitlyn thought. *In ten years, he's never even sent me a postcard. Not that I wanted to hear from him....*

She supposed a lot of other people were going to be wondering, too. People in Springhill didn't forget, she told herself morosely. And though no one had brought the subject up to Kaitlyn for a year or more, it was foolish to think that it had faded entirely into the past, for it was far too interesting to be forgotten altogether. The simple fact was that nearly everyone had expected, back then, that someday Kaitlyn Ross would marry Penn Caldwell. Nearly everyone in Springhill—including Kaitlyn.

And they had all felt sorry for her when, after the tragedy, it turned out that Penn didn't feel the same way at all,

and he went abruptly off to roam the world instead of set-
tling down.

So now Penn was back. And everyone in Springhill was
going to be watching....

But not for long, she reminded herself. The weekend—
maybe three or four days—and he would be gone again.
That was the one guaranteed thing about Penn. He'd never
stuck to anything in his life.

THE LIMOUSINE DRIVER had orders to take his time trans-
porting the newlyweds from church to country club, so
that Kaitlyn had a few minutes to be certain that everything was in place for the reception and that no careless
waiter had fallen into the cake or managed to clog up the
champagne fountain. All of that was really the caterer's
problem, of course, but if it didn't go right, the blame
would ultimately come to rest on Kaitlyn. That was why
people hired a wedding consultant in the first place, she
reminded herself—because they wanted smooth, elegant
perfection in everything from orchids to champagne punch
to photographs. And because that way they'd have someone to blame if things went wrong, she reflected wryly.

The dancing was well under way, and she was reminding the band leader of his promise to play all sorts of music, not just the youngest generation's favorite kind, when
the groom came up beside her with a courtly bow. "May I
have this dance?"

"Neil, you know I don't dance at these parties—there
are too many things to keep an eye on."

He looked around, his brow furrowed. "Like what?"

"Like the waiters who are serving the cake."

"They look perfectly capable to me. Come on, Kaitlyn." He gestured to the band leader, who smiled mischie-
vously and struck up a waltz. Before Kaitlyn could protest,

she was in the middle of the dance floor, and Neil was saying earnestly, "Besides, you're by far the best dancer here—it would be a waste to leave you on the sidelines. I'm surprised Marcus hasn't dragged you out here by the hair."

"Marcus knows my rules. Business is—"

"But this is business," Neil objected. "It will be the only chance I get to tell you privately how grateful I am for all your help in restraining Angela's mother. If she'd had her way, this would have been a three-ring circus."

Kaitlyn privately agreed, but she said, diplomatically, "Actually, all I did was carry out Angela's wishes."

"Now what about my wishes? It looks to me as if everything is running smoothly, so you're to enjoy yourself for the rest of the evening—and that's an order. You're our guest as well as the coordinator, you know."

She shook her head. "Just this dance, Neil."

There was a tap on his shoulder. "Go waltz with your bride, Neil, and let me say hello to Kaitlyn."

It had been ten years since she had heard that voice, and she would never forget hearing it raised in anger—fury, actually, mixed with frustration and pain.... But now there was only lazy good humor as Penn turned to her. "Dance with me for old times' sake, Kitten?"

Kitten. He had called her that, often, but she had almost forgotten how soft and sultry he could make it sound.

She contemplated, for a moment, stamping her foot down on his and walking off the floor—just for old times' sake. But she was precisely in the middle of the ballroom, and there were too many eyes. People were watching, all right. She couldn't cause that sort of scene in the middle of Angela's wedding, no matter how much Penn deserved it.

So she raised one hand to his shoulder and put the other hesitantly into his and let him swing her off across the floor. The last time he had held her—

Stop it, she told herself firmly. *You're not going to start all that nonsense. It doesn't matter anymore.*

"My name is not Kitten," she said. Her voice was a little throatier than usual.

Penn shook his head sadly. "Don't tell me you've turned into a radical feminist while I've been gone."

"Of course I haven't."

"I beg your pardon. A radical feminist wouldn't be making a business of arranging fancy weddings, would she? She'd be more likely to be outside the church with a picket sign, protesting that the ancient ritual demeans women."

"If your definition of a radical feminist includes opposing weddings," Kaitlyn said sweetly, "you're far more of one than I am—aren't you?"

His gray eyes turned silvery with laughter. "You haven't let those claws get dull, have you? Are there really enough people getting married in Springhill to keep a wedding consultant busy?"

She nodded. "It looks that way. It will take time to build up my business—I've only been doing this for eight months—so I do other parties, as well. But I've got some wedding bookings for almost a year from now."

Penn looked disbelievingly. "And these people all want to make public spectacles of themselves just so they can be married?"

"They want nice weddings," she corrected. "And these days not only does the bride have a job that keeps her from making all the arrangements herself, but her mother does, too. So it's a perfect niche for an expert who can coordinate everything and leave the family free to enjoy themselves at the party."

"The expert being you. Self-appointed, of course."

Kaitlyn frowned at the tone of his voice, but she said firmly, "That's right. And it's not so crazy; I've been helping my friends with their weddings forever, unofficially, so I certainly know what I'm doing now that I've gone professional."

Penn whistled admiringly. "Nice work if you can get it. I just hope you can keep your clients convinced that you're indispensable."

The jab annoyed her. "At least be honest, Penn. It isn't just weddings you think are unnecessary—it's marriage, too. In fact, with the way you feel about the whole concept, I'm surprised you even showed up for Angela's wedding."

"First one I've attended in years."

"Well," she said with sweet sarcasm, "perhaps that accounts for why you were so rude you didn't even bother to send back your response card."

He shook his head. "Oh, no—the invitation just took so long to catch up with me that there wasn't time. I've been moving around a bit."

That came as no surprise. Good old Penn, she thought. The grass was always greener on the other side of the fence.... For the first time, she found herself wondering if he would have been that way if it hadn't been for the tragedy. Had the horrible accident that had swept away his family caused this restlessness in him, or had it simply released a tendency that had always been there?

"Besides, I'm not opposed to marriage for Angela," he added, with wide-eyed earnestness and emphasis on the name.

"Merely for yourself. I suppose some things never change." She bit her tongue, a second too late.

"Don't tell me you're still holding a grudge over that, Kitten. Just because I didn't want to marry you—"

"Of course I'm not holding a grudge," Kaitlyn said crisply. "If I'd actually married you, I'd probably be a widow by now—serving time in prison for your murder."

"No doubt." The idea didn't seem to disturb him. "See what trouble I saved us all by refusing to indulge your little whim?"

She deliberately missed a step and kicked him in the ankle, then gave him a pseudoapologetic smile as he protested. "I seem to be a little tired," she explained. The band leader must have been getting even with her for reminding him of his promise to mix the musical styles— she'd never heard a waltz go on so long.

"Too tired to waltz? You? I don't believe it. I used to go off to sleep every night thinking about waltzing with you, Kitten."

Her breath caught for just an instant in her throat, and then she forced herself to release it.

"That was when I was in the jungle, of course," he added practically. "There wasn't much else to think about."

This time he sidestepped her toe, and smiled contentedly down at her. "What's happened to Springhill, by the way? I was driving around this morning and I practically got lost."

She was relieved that he didn't seem to want to rehash the past anymore. She certainly didn't; it was long over, and even an apology for the way he'd treated her wouldn't help now—though she couldn't think of anything less likely than the idea of Penn actually apologizing!

"Whole new sections of this town have sprung up from nowhere since I left," he added. "And there's a For Sale sign on your old house."

For an instant, her heart fluttered at the thought of Penn driving past to see what her house looked like after his long absence. The memories it held must have been important to him, after all, if he'd done that....

Then the quivery rhythm settled back to normal. It would have been hard to avoid seeing it, she told herself, if he'd been driving around town for longer than half an hour. The Ross house wasn't a grand one, but it was located on a prominent corner.

There was nothing special about that house, she told herself, certainly not his memories of it.

She shrugged. "After Dad died last year—"

Penn caught his breath, and his hand tightened momentarily on hers. "I hadn't heard that, Kaitlyn."

"I don't know how you'd expect to," she said sharply. "If you're moving around so much—" She stopped abruptly. There was nothing so awful about his sympathy, was there? Certainly he knew how it felt to lose a father.

"I'm very sorry," Penn said quietly.

"Thank you, it was a long illness, and it was very hard on Mother. She's decided she'd like a change, so if she gets her price for the house, she'll take an apartment in one of the new complexes that are going up."

"And you, Kitten?" It was little more than a whisper. "What will you do?"

But the music died softly away just then. It was a relief to step back from him, and yet her feet didn't quite want to stop moving, to cease following the rhythms learned so long ago and so well.

They had ended up at the edge of the ballroom, and she saw, from the corner of her eye, a man rising from a table nearby. "Kaitlyn, I had no idea you'd changed your mind about dancing. I'm sorry, dear. If I'd known—"

She was feeling suddenly drained, almost too exhausted to turn around. "Marcus," she said. "Have you met Penn, yet? You should."

She couldn't see Marcus's face, but she could almost feel the tension in him—no, surely that was too strong a word. What reason could there be for Marcus to feel uneasy at an ordinary introduction?

"Penn, this is my friend Marcus Wainwright," she murmured.

Penn seized Marcus's hand and shook it enthusiastically. "I'm delighted to meet you. And just what is your line of work, Mr. Wainwright?"

Marcus looked a little put out at the eager approach. "I'm the president of TurfMaster. We make lawn tractors and equipment to maintain golf courses—that sort of thing." Marcus sounded a bit distracted; Kaitlyn didn't realize why until she saw him eyeing her right hand, which was still firmly clasped in Penn's left. She hadn't noticed till then that the man had never completely released her after the waltz had ended. She pulled away as unobtrusively as she could.

"And you?" Marcus asked. "What is it you do?"

Penn said cheerfully. "Oh, I'm self-employed."

Kaitlyn's jaw dropped. "Now that's the most misleading—"

"Is it, Kitten?" Penn didn't sound interested.

"Kitten?" Marcus repeated, as if the word tasted sour. "Her name is—"

"Yes, I know. But I've always called her Kitten." Penn didn't continue, but there was a soft note in his voice that invited inquiry.

Kaitlyn glared at him, and then realized that to react to that sort of teasing was the best way to guarantee it went on. So she turned the glare into a parody of a fond smile. "Of course it's misleading to say Penn's self-employed— he's independently rich. Or at least he used to be. Penn's family owned TurfMaster, Marcus. It wasn't called that, though."

"Oh, of course. I seem to recall . . ." It was casual, as if now that he knew where to classify Penn, Marcus no longer cared. "Your name must be—" His brow wrinkled, but it couldn't have been plainer that trying to remember Penn's name was no more than a social nicety.

Marcus was abruptly brushed aside, as easily if he was a cardboard cutout, by a big man in a tuxedo who threw both arms around Penn. "Caldwell, you mysterious old creature—we all thought you'd fallen off the edge of the earth. Nobody's heard from you in a year, dammit!"

Penn returned the hug. "Didn't you get my picture postcards from Caracas? I took the photos of the sights myself and had them printed up."

"Damn, it's good to see you, Penn. You're staying for a while, aren't you? You have to. You can be the best man at my wedding a week from today."

Penn patted him sympathetically on the back. "You've caught the fatal bug, too, my friend?"

Kaitlyn thought it was time to be firm. "You already have a best man, Karl," she pointed out.

Karl shrugged. "Only my brother. He'll understand." He draped an arm across Penn's shoulders. "I'd have sent you an invitation if I'd known where to mail it. Did you say Caracas? You mean Venezuela? Well, if that isn't something—'' The two of them wandered off across the ballroom.

"It's a relief to be rid of him," Marcus said. "It's so unpleasant to have a drunk hanging around."

Annoyed as she was at Penn, Kaitlyn couldn't square it with her conscience to let that go unchallenged. "He wasn't drunk."

"Oh? He was certainly acting strangely."

"That's just Penn. He's a volatile personality."

"That seems an understatement. How did you ever manage to meet him? I can't quite see you being friends."

It was a long time ago, she reminded herself. So why bother Marcus with the details? *You certainly haven't told him about all the other people you've dated, so why explain Penn?*

Because Penn was different... She quickly squashed that thought.

"Well, you know how things are when you're a teenager," she said vaguely. "There were half a dozen of us who went everywhere in a pack, especially in the summer, when we all spent weeks up at Sapphire Lake. And—"

"And this guy was the joker in the pack?"

Kaitlyn smiled. "Something like that."

Marcus gave her shoulder a reassuring squeeze. "There's one in every crowd, isn't there, who ends up as nutty as a chocolate bar? It's fortunate we don't have to keep them around all the time, just because they were once—in a sense—friends."

He pulled out a chair and Kaitlyn sank into it gratefully. So much for Penn, she thought; he'd been dismissed to the outer darkness, where he belonged. Marcus had such a way of putting things in perspective!

He snapped his fingers at a passing waiter and got Kaitlyn a glass of club soda. "Why on earth would he call you

Kitten, anyway?'' he asked curiously. ''You're not exactly the frail and fluffy little helpless sort that name brings to mind.''

She drew in a quick breath, surprised that he'd brought it up again. Oxygen collided with carbonation, and it took half a minute before she could answer. ''Oh, Penn doesn't think I'm fluffy and helpless, either. The nickname is because some of the little kids at the lake couldn't pronounce my name, so they called me Kitten instead. Penn just picked it up.'' Of course, the way Penn said it, the name was never quite so innocent, she reflected. But there was certainly no point in telling Marcus *that!* ''A bunch of the others in the group did, too.''

''I've certainly never heard you called that.'' He sounded a little grumpy.

She smiled. ''Because I've spent the past ten years eradicating the habit.''

''And he didn't get the message? I can't say I'm surprised. He struck me as an insensitive sort.''

She sipped her drink and thought about letting it go at that. Then honesty made her say, ''Well, he wasn't around, so he could hardly know how much I grew to hate it, could he? Marcus, I've got to check on how things are going in the kitchen. And it's time for Angela to toss her bouquet.''

He nodded. ''You know, Kaitlyn, these parties were a lot more fun before you started masterminding all of them.''

''That's the drawback of the business, I'm afraid. But I like it so much better than selling clothes, or teaching.'' She gave him a quick smile and let her hand rest on his shoulder. ''That's not a very impressive record, is it? Twenty-eight years old, and I've embarked on my third career! But this time I really like what I'm doing, Marcus.''

"Then you'd better go and do it," he said glumly. He reached for another glass of champagne as she went off to supervise the rest of the traditions.

Neil turned the removal of the bride's garter into an elaborate ceremony, and heckled the crowd until all his unmarried friends were out on the dance floor hoping to catch it. Almost all of them, Kaitlyn amended. Penn and Karl had retreated to a corner, and from the bits of talk she overhead as she made her regular supervising rounds of the hall, Penn seemed to be trying to convince his friend to choose the Sahara Desert for a honeymoon spot. Kaitlyn rolled her eyes and hoped fervently that word of *that* didn't come to the ears of Karl's fiancée—Sabrina was a lovely girl, but she was not known for her sense of humor. And now, with her wedding less than a week away, Kaitlyn couldn't really blame her.

A tiny headache nagged just behind Kaitlyn's eyebrows. Marcus was right; weddings and celebrations had been a whole lot more fun before she started doing all the work personally. But there were drawbacks to every job, and advantages, as well, Kaitlyn reminded herself. She loved what she did, most of the time. It was only late at night, after a very long day, that she had even the slightest regrets.

Eventually it came to an end; the bride and groom drove off in their garishly decorated car, the caterer's men packed up the rubbish and disappeared, and all that was left were the decorations, a bit tired and bedraggled and quite able to wait for morning when the florist would retrieve them.

"I'll follow you home," Marcus said, as Kaitlyn gathered up the guest book and the pair of gilt sandals someone had left in the ladies' lounge—how on earth had the owner managed to lose them? "Just to be sure that you're all right."

It gave her a warm little glow; it was comforting that Marcus was so cautious about her safety. Springhill was certainly not New York City, but it was still pleasant to be looked after and treated with care.

But he didn't just see her home; his Mercedes pulled into the driveway behind her little car, and he got out.

Kaitlyn said, too tired to mind that she sounded a bit rude, "Marcus, it's awfully late. And I'm exhausted."

"I won't come in; your mother will have settled down for the night. But I would like to talk to you a minute, Kaitlyn." He gave her a strained smile. "It seems we don't have much chance to talk lately. You're always busy."

She couldn't argue with that. A great deal of her work fell into the evenings—the long planning sessions with her clients, at least. And when she wasn't tied up with business, it seemed that Marcus was. TurfMaster was a big operation now—under corporate management it had far outgrown the regional enterprise that Penn's father had built—and it kept Marcus busy.

She led the way to the old wicker swing, suspended with heavy chains from the porch ceiling. The bolts that held it secure creaked a little as the swing began to rock. It formed a soft cricketlike rhythm, which was the last thing Kaitlyn needed if she was going to stay awake. She sat up very straight.

"I was going to ask you this at the reception," Marcus said. "Then your friend the maniac came along, and— well, that's beside the point, isn't it? Kaitlyn—" He turned a little toward her, and folded her hand into his.

Kaitlyn tried to smother a yawn.

Marcus said wryly, "It's selfish of me perhaps to feel I have to ask this minute, but I do, you see. You introduced me as your friend tonight, but I want the right to be more than that. Will you marry me, darling?"

All the sleepiness disappeared in the whisk of an eyelash. Kaitlyn couldn't remember ever before being so suddenly and so dramatically wakened—unless it was the time she'd fallen asleep on the beach at the lake, and rather than drag her out of the sunlight Penn had dumped a picnic cooler full of ice over her bikini-clad body....

That sort of wandering thinking was not the way one ought to respond to a proposal of marriage, she told herself firmly. *Get a grip on yourself, Kaitlyn Ross!* It wasn't as if this was any tremendous surprise, after all. She'd been seeing Marcus for a year, and she'd been half-expecting this question for months now....

She opened her mouth to accept his proposal, to say that she would be delighted to become his wife. And instead, she heard herself saying, almost hoarsely, "Marcus, it's such a big decision. I—I want a chance to think about it. Please..."

CHAPTER TWO

MARCUS WAS SO STARTLED that he almost fell out of the porch swing. Kaitlyn didn't blame him; she was stunned herself by what she had said. She hadn't been dating anyone else for more than six months, so she shouldn't have had any doubts about giving Marcus an answer as soon as he'd asked the question—or of what that answer would be.

He chuckled a little, self-consciously. "Surely you're not giving me the shy maiden's routine, Kaitlyn? Crying, 'This is such a surprise.' "

She shook her head. "It's not sudden," she said, and then realized that wasn't the most tactful of responses, either. "And yet it *is* a big step, Marcus—and I haven't thought it through. I enjoy being with you, and I like you, but when it comes to making it permanent—"

You're getting in deeper and deeper, she warned herself. *You've already gone from thoughtless to inconsiderate, and if you're not careful you'll be verging on rude!* She added, miserably, "Please say you understand. It's just that I want to be very sure, for both our sakes."

The line of Marcus's mouth had gone tight and his voice was brisk. "Of course I understand, Kaitlyn. It's my fault, no doubt, for not waiting till you were rested. I'll see you tomorrow, then?"

She smiled in agreement and then remembered her schedule. "I have to be at the club while the rental people pick up the extra tables and chairs, and to check on the florist.''

''That surely won't take all day,'' he said, and stood up. ''I'll call you.''

She nodded, and watched as he crossed the porch, almost too tired to react to the suddenness of his departure. Then she jumped up and followed him. ''Marcus, aren't you going to kiss me good night?''

''I thought perhaps I wasn't invited to do so at the moment.''

''Don't be silly,'' she whispered, and tipped her head against the fluted porch pillar to look down at him. He caught his breath and came back to the top of the steps, and kissed her with his customary enthusiasm—or was there a little restraint there? Just the slightest bit of hesitation, of uncertainty?

She was still leaning against the pillar with one hand raised to provide a buffer between her cheek and the chalky white paint when he left. She watched without moving until the Mercedes's taillights vanished down the dimly lit boulevard.

Time for bed, she told herself. But with a sigh, she went back to the porch swing instead and dropped into its comforting cushions. She could lie down on it, if she bent her knees and propped her feet against the arm.

''Idiot,'' she muttered. ''That's not the way you've always expected you'd react to a proposal.''

Certainly it wasn't the way she had anticipated answering Marcus, and the sudden hesitation bothered her. She certainly knew by now how much she liked him, and she knew—for he had told her—that he was very fond of her. If someone had whispered in her ear tonight that Marcus loved her and that he was about to ask her to marry him, she would have been pleased, but not surprised. No one in

Springhill would have been startled, for they had all assumed that sooner or later—

She thought that over, morosely. *Everyone expects it.* Was that the problem?

Once before, everybody in Springhill had assumed the same sort of thing—except with a different man. That time they had all been disappointed, and the outpouring of awkward sympathy had been as difficult to deal with as Penn's own rejection. Was that old wound still throbbing, deep under the surface? Was it possible, she wondered, that she had been holding herself back from truly loving Marcus just because *Penn* hadn't been able or willing to make a commitment?

"Idiot," she repeated. "Double-dipped idiot, if that's what you've been doing!"

The breeze rippled through the spirea hedge in front of the house and toyed with a strand of her honey-brown hair, using it to tickle her cheek. June's warm evening breezes always reminded her of that last sweet summertime, now ten long years ago....

She had been in the final two weeks of classes, ready to graduate from high school in the spring, when Penn came home from his first year at the university. She'd been sitting in the porch swing that Saturday morning, with a textbook, trying to concentrate on the Cavalier poets, when he came whistling up the walk. Just seeing him again, with the sunshine gleaming on his black hair and turning his eyes to silver, had made her heart ache with gladness. And love. It hadn't been an easy year, with him so far away. But that was over now; in the autumn, she would follow him to the university, and they would always be together. They hadn't talked about it exactly, but in Kaitlyn's mind at least it was all very clear.

There had been no hint, then, that the long sweet summertime of her youth was almost gone—that perfect time when all things were possible because she was young and in love. The world itself was fresh and shiny, with no hint that it was about to shift ominously on its axis.

But then, one hot day in July, Penn's world had come crashing down—and Kaitlyn's had begun to crumble, as well, though she didn't even know it herself for a matter of weeks....

She'd been getting her teeth cleaned when her dentist said, "Terrible about the Caldwells, isn't it?"

Her heart had seemed to shudder to a stop, and she'd managed to mumble through a mouthful of gritty abrasive, "What do you mean? They're fishing up on Lake Superior this week—"

She could still feel the sick weakness that had washed over her as he repeated what his last patient had just told him about the accident, and the story that was filtering back to Springhill—of the drunk in the speedboat who had rammed into the side of the Caldwells' chartered cabin cruiser that morning and split it nearly in two.

"It can't be true," she had whispered, almost desperate in her denial. "You know how stories grow wilder as they're passed along!"

But it had been true, and by evening the whole town was talking about it, and the fact that both of Penn's parents had been below deck—and now they were dead.

Penn himself had been at the wheel of the cabin cruiser. He had been thrown clear in the collision, to inhale lake water and spilled fuel, to try to keep himself afloat and dodge the drifting bits of wreckage, until he was picked up by a boater who had witnessed the accident. Still bruised and bandaged, he had brought his parents home a few days later and stood quietly beside their grave, the only survivor not only of a horrible accident but of a family line.

They had said—the people of Springhill—that he was made of strong stuff to take it like that. Later, of course, they changed their minds and announced that he'd been too calm, too passive. It had been unnatural, they said; some kind of backlash had been inevitable. They had known it was coming all along.

But weeks had gone by before the inevitable had happened. . . .

The screen door squeaked as it opened halfway. Audrey Ross leaned out and said, quietly, "Kaitlyn? Is that you?"

"Yes, Mom." She sat up, rubbing her upper arms almost unconsciously, still shivering at the memories. The swing creaked as it stirred under her weight.

Audrey came across the porch soft footed, belting her terry robe. "You're alone? I thought I heard Penn. Did he bring you home?"

"No, Marcus did."

"Oh. Of course." Audrey yawned. "I suppose I was half asleep, and must have heard the porch swing creak, and it reminded me of all the nights you and Penn would sit out here till the wee hours." She settled herself on the end of the swing. "And of how your father would come downstairs and ask Penn what time it was, and Penn would politely tell him—"

"And then he still wouldn't take the hint to go home," Kaitlyn finished.

Audrey smiled a little. "I suppose I'm just feeling more sentimental than usual," she murmured. "Stephanie told me tonight she's had an offer on the house. She'll bring it over in the morning for me to consider."

"On Sunday? Does that woman work all the time?"

"She said the buyers are coming from out of town, so I'm sure they're anxious to get an answer." Audrey yawned again. "I hope it's a good offer—I must say it would be a relief to have it all decided. The lawn needs to be mowed, I see, and the little Benton boy is away."

"Again?"

"Some sort of camp-out, I think. I wonder who I can get to take care of it. It's not like it was when you were in school, is it, dear? Then there were all kinds of young men hanging about all the time."

"And every one of them could be bribed with cookies or apple pie or pocket money."

"Speaking of young men," Audrey mused, "I wonder..."

Kaitlyn laughed. "Whether Marcus would consider this lawn as a sort of test plot for TurfMaster's new equipment? I'll ask him, Mother, but—"

"No, that's not what I meant at all. I wonder if Penn might take care of it."

Kaitlyn bit her lip. Then, very quietly, she said, "All that was a long time ago, Mom."

She thought for a moment that her mother hadn't heard, but finally Audrey said distantly, "Yes. I know it was, dear. Don't you think that by now—" She sighed, and Kaitlyn braced herself, but instead Audrey said merely, "I always liked Penn, you know."

"I know you did. I'll try to find time to do the mowing myself. But for now, don't you think you'd better go to bed, Mother? You'll have to be on your toes when you look at that offer in the morning."

Audrey pushed herself up from the swing. "Kaitlyn, what really did go wrong between you and Penn?" she asked almost hesitantly. "If it was one of those silly misunderstandings that happen now and then— Well, you must remember the terrible shock he'd had, darling.''

"I never forgot it, Mother. And we didn't have just a silly misunderstanding. But it's too late to talk about it."

Audrey seemed to understand that she wasn't referring to the clock, but to the calendar. "It's never too late, darling. And if it would make you feel better..."

The idea made Kaitlyn shiver. Spill out the embarrassing details to her mother now? After all these years of keeping them to herself? "This time it's too late," she said firmly.

"It's up to you, of course. But if you ever change your mind, dear—"

Kaitlyn nodded, but as soon as Audrey was out of hearing range, she muttered, "No thanks, Mother. I certainly wouldn't like to tell you about it."

But it wasn't only the unpleasant idea of sharing her shame that was keeping her quiet, she realized. It was unwillingness to cause Audrey hurt. Her mother hadn't just liked Penn; she'd adored him. Why ruin that, too? Why take away Audrey's good memories—when it was far too late to change what had happened that summer ten long years ago?

IT WAS A PERFECT sunny Sunday morning, with the golf course filled with players, swimmers already splashing in the pool and joggers out on the paths, when Kaitlyn drove home from the country club. The rented equipment was safely on its way back to the warehouse, and the florist had retrieved all of his belongings. She could close the books on another successful event, and have a day or two of peace before the tension began to build for Sabrina Hart's wedding next weekend.

That's a joke, she told herself. The tension's been on a steady upward climb for weeks already. I don't think it can build much more—or that I can forget the whole thing for a couple of days, either. I'd better talk to the woman at the bridal shop tomorrow about those tuxedos. . . .

This would be the biggest wedding she'd handled in her eight months in business, and Kaitlyn was counting on it to make her reputation not only in Springhill but throughout the whole corner of the state. If Sabrina's wedding came off smoothly, all six hundred guests would be impressed. And if it didn't—

She closed her eyes briefly at the nightmare vision of the caterer's van running a Stop sign and Sabrina's wedding cake ending up as a crumbly stain on an intersection.

Nothing would dare happen to that cake, she told herself. She simply wouldn't let anything go wrong.

Stephanie Kendall's black Jaguar was in the driveway, so Kaitlyn parked her car on Belle Vista Avenue in front of the house and strolled up the sidewalk. She was in no hurry to get inside; either the offer to buy the house was satisfactory or it wasn't, and in any case it was not her decision to make.

Not that there wasn't a twinge deep in her heart at the idea of giving up the house she had grown up in. But it wasn't her home any longer, she reminded herself—not really. She had moved back in with her parents during her father's last illness in order to give Audrey all the help she could, and she had only stayed on after his death because her mother had been so desperately lost and lonely. But those days were past; Audrey was coping with her grief, and Kaitlyn was looking forward to being back on her own again.

She stopped at the foot of the front steps and looked up at the white clapboard house with the dark blue shutters.

It was big and square and solid and unpretentious, one of a row of dwellings built by middle-class merchants at the turn of the century. Like any house of that vintage, it needed the loving touch of a handyman, constantly keeping it in repair. Kaitlyn hadn't realized until after her father was no longer able to putter about the house just how much he'd been doing, or how difficult it would be for her mother to manage alone. When Audrey had first tentatively brought up the subject of selling, Kaitlyn had been almost relieved.

In the kitchen, Audrey was refilling a coffee mug for the lovely redhead who sat at the table. Beside her on the polished surface lay a manila folder; papers peeked out of the corners of it as if they had been carelessly pushed aside.

Kaitlyn glanced at the folder. "No deal, hmm?" she hazarded. "That's a shame. Hello, Stephanie."

The redhead gave her a brilliant smile. "Of course it's a deal. At least it will be as soon as Audrey signs the papers."

"Then what's holding you up, Mother? The price?" Kaitlyn got herself a mug.

Audrey filled it. "Not exactly. It's a good offer. But they want possession of the house in two weeks."

Kaitlyn choked on her coffee. "That's a bit brisk, isn't it?"

Stephanie said solemnly, "It's faster than usual, yes. But the buyers are a young couple with two small children and another on the way, so they want to get settled somewhere and stay there. They've already sold their old house, and he starts to work in Springhill in three weeks, so—"

"It's impossible," Audrey said firmly. "I can't go through an entire house and sort and pack in two weeks. All of Kaitlyn's baby clothes are still in the attic, for heaven's sake. Stephanie, I can't be out of here in two weeks. Two months, maybe. If they could wait just a little longer..."

Stephanie's gaze was understanding. "I'll tell them. But I have to be frank, Audrey. I don't think they'll wait. There were a couple of houses they didn't like as well, but they're available now." She set her cup aside and reached for the folder. "Thanks for the coffee. I'll let you know."

Audrey released a long breath and said, "I don't see what else I can do. I don't have an apartment, or—"

Kaitlyn pulled up a chair. "Now hold on a minute. Let's not do anything rash. You said this is a good offer, Stephanie?"

The redhead nodded. "It's the first one I've had in a while that's every dollar of the asking price."

Kaitlyn whistled.

"These are reasonable people," Stephanie went on. "They know it's an imposition to ask you to move so quickly, so they're willing to pay more."

Kaitlyn stirred her coffee slowly. "Is anyone else likely to come up with that price?"

"It's possible," Stephanie conceded. "But not likely, and it might take a while. We priced it on the high side, you know."

Kaitlyn turned to her mother. "Do you want to sell the house, or not?"

Audrey looked at her as if she'd suddenly sprouted an extra nose. "Of course I do. I put it on the market, didn't I?"

"Then I think you should take this offer."

"But all the work," Audrey wailed. "In two weeks!"

"It might be easier that way. Ripping off a surgical bandage hurts less than picking at it. I'll help, Mother."

When? she asked herself. Between Sabrina Hart's wedding this weekend, and Laura McCarthy's on the following Saturday... June, she thought in irritation. Why does every woman in the world want to be married in June?

Stephanie seemed to be reading her mind. "We'll figure something out. With the extra money, Audrey, you could have the movers put everything in storage until you're ready to settle somewhere, and sort it all out then. You can even stack it in my garage, for heaven's sake."

Audrey looked at her daughter for a long moment, and then back to Stephanie.

"It's very natural to have doubts at this stage, Audrey," Stephanie said gently. "It doesn't mean you'll regret selling."

Audrey sighed. "Where do I sign?"

Stephanie didn't move. "If you want to think it over, I can ask if they'll wait till tomorrow."

Audrey shook her head. "No, you're right—both of you. I know I've got to sell this house, and it wouldn't be any easier to get rid of things if I had a year—I'd just keep putting it off." She reached for the folder and a pen.

Stephanie handed over the duplicate copies to be signed as well, and it was done. The official contract went back into the folder and was tucked safely into Stephanie's briefcase.

Kaitlyn walked out to the Jaguar with her. "Thanks for being so patient with Mother," she murmured.

Stephanie smiled. "Oh, I understand what she's going through. When I sold the first little house I'd ever owned, I cried for days, even though it made no sense at all to be upset." She waved and called out, "Hello, Marcus!"

Kaitlyn swung around to see him crossing the street to join them. "I was on my way home from golfing and saw your car," he told Kaitlyn. "So I stopped to ask about your plans for the rest of the day, darling."

Kaitlyn tipped her face up so he could kiss her cheek. "I haven't made any. Except for mowing the lawn."

"In that case," Stephanie said, "come up to Sapphire Lake to our cabin this evening. It's nothing elaborate, but I've invited all the old gang."

The old gang, Kaitlyn thought. It wasn't an unusual invitation; relatively few of that crowd of friends had remained in Springhill, but they still saw a great deal of one another. Last week the invitation wouldn't have given her a twinge. But today, she could think of a hundred things she'd rather do than go up to the lake with all the old gang—

Oh, be honest, she told herself. It isn't the old gang that bothers you, but one particular member of it.

And she'd just told Stephanie that she had no plans that would keep her from attending.

Before she could find her voice, Marcus said, "That sounds like fun. Kaitlyn was telling me just last night about your younger days."

"Please don't make us sound like senior citizens," Stephanie begged. "I can count on you, then? It will be just like old times—hot dogs on the bonfire, and maybe a moonlight swim."

Just like old times. That, Kaitlyn thought, was exactly what she was afraid of.

MARCUS DIDN'T TAKE his eyes off the twisting gravel road that led back into the hills north of Springhill to Sapphire Lake. He frowned as gravel kept pinging off the underside of his car, despite his cautious speed. "So that means you've got just two weeks to find a place to live?"

"Actually," she said calmly, "it's worse than that. We've got two weeks to find *two* places to live. I love my mother dearly, but it's been hard enough to share a house with her. An apartment would be impossible.''

"Does she know that?"

"Absolutely. We talked it over before she listed the house for sale. It can't be that difficult, Marcus. There are a dozen new apartment complexes."

"That may be true, but I think you're overestimating the quality of what's available," he said morosely. "Don't forget how long I looked before I found a satisfactory place. I dread the day I have to start shopping for a house." A tinge of color climbed into his cheeks, and he darted a look at Kaitlyn. "I'm sorry, dear. I certainly didn't mean to imply that I've changed my mind about marriage since last night. I was only saying—"

"That the housing market in this town is impossible right now, if you're a buyer. I know; Stephanie's told me." Kaitlyn tried to conceal a sigh of relief as the car topped a hill that overlooked the small, brilliant blue lake. In two more minutes they'd be down at the Kendalls' cabin, and there would be no more chance for private discussions, or difficult questions for which she still had no answers. She simply hadn't had time today to give Marcus's proposal the thought it deserved—but she didn't exactly want to tell him that he hadn't been at the top of her list.

She peered down at the lake. The air was so still that the water looked almost like a mirror—or the polished surface of a gemstone. "Doesn't it look like a sapphire, with the pine trees holding it firm in some gigantic ring?"

Marcus chuckled. "You have such a romantic view of the world, Kaitlyn. It's a nice little lake, but hardly the most beautiful one I've ever seen."

"But it's *our* lake," she said, feeling a bit stubborn about the fact. "And it's close enough to home to enjoy, which makes it a great deal more beautiful, in my opinion.''

The Kendalls' summer home sprawled across the gentle hillside just fifty feet or so above the shore line, one of a dozen set next to the water. It was one of the newer buildings on the lake, but the architect had studiously copied the best features of the older ones, complete with a screened sleeping porch and a fieldstone fireplace large enough to roast a whole pig. Down on the sand, a pile of driftwood had already been gathered, waiting for the cooler air that would come with twilight.

Stephanie had said she'd invited the old gang, but she obviously hadn't limited her invitations to long-time friends, for there was a row of cars on each side of the narrow graveled road that wound around the lake. Kaitlyn relaxed a little. This would be no intimate reunion, that was sure—there were far too many people here who would be bored to tears by the rehashing of old memories.

There was a chorus of feminine greetings from the huge deck overhanging the beach as they came around the corner of the cabin. Kaitlyn waved back, set her wicker basket down on a picnic table, which was already groaning under the weight of various snack foods, and they climbed the shallow stairs to join the others on the deck. ''Where are all the guys?'' Kaitlyn asked, realizing that Marcus was the only male in sight.

''They went to inspect Penn's cabin,'' Stephanie said. She leaned over the deck rail to check on the half-dozen children who were playing in the wading pool below.

Kaitlyn was eyeing a weather-beaten building far down the beach. ''I'm surprised you aren't with them.''

''I wasn't invited.''

''But if he's thinking of selling—''

"If that's what he's got in mind, he certainly hasn't told me about it."

Kaitlyn chewed her lip. *Don't jump to conclusions,* she told herself. *He's within a hundred yards of the place, so of course it makes sense to look it over and be certain it's still holding together, no matter what he plans to do with it.*

"I don't see why he'd want to hold on to it any longer," she said. "He's already let it stand there empty for ten years."

"Not my business," Stephanie murmured. She reached for a handful of corn chips from a basket that stood nearby.

And it wasn't Kaitlyn's, either. But the fact was, she reflected, that she was a bit hypersensitive about that cabin. She'd better cut that out before someone started to suspect there might be a reason.

The front door of the Caldwell cabin opened, and a half-dozen men emerged. Kaitlyn turned around just as a burst of laughter came from a corner of the deck, and she wondered for one instant if she looked guilty—hanging over the rail like that, staring down the beach—so guilty that she had become a source of entertainment.

Then one of the women said, "Remember the night Stephanie slid down the grand stairway at the hotel on a pizza pan?" and a couple of others began to giggle like the carefree teenagers they'd once been, and Kaitlyn relaxed.

How different they'd all become, she thought, since the days when they used to come to Sapphire Lake to spend the summers! It had happened so gradually that she seldom noticed it. But she wondered what Penn thought, seeing the changes in them all at once....

And here I am thinking about Penn again, she reflected.

Stephanie crossed the deck and sat down on the wooden bench that formed part of the rail. "Shall we just forget about the pizza pan? At least I didn't turn up at the senior prom on roller skates and almost get expelled."

"I didn't almost get expelled," Kaitlyn protested. "I just got a lecture on not letting—" she almost said *Penn,* and caught herself at the last second "—other people lead me into trouble." Marcus's eyebrows climbed slightly, but Kaitlyn wasn't watching. She dropped onto the bench beside Stephanie.

Metal shrieked against wood as the seat parted from the rail and dumped both women onto the deck floor. Stephanie swore and then looked anxiously over her shoulder to see whether the children in the wading pool were within hearing distance.

"It must have been the extra Danish I had for breakfast," Kaitlyn lamented. "Sorry about your bench, Steph."

The knot of men down on the sand had obviously heard the commotion. Penn called, "Is it safe to come up, or are you going to dismantle the rest of the deck, too?"

"Damned builders," Stephanie muttered. "They don't have to do quality work these days because there just aren't enough of them to go around, so even the incompetent ones stay busy." She scrambled up and tried to peer under the broken bench.

Marcus bent over Kaitlyn anxiously. "Are you hurt?"

"Only my pride." She held a hand up to him for assistance.

"Perhaps you shouldn't move just yet," he warned. "Not until we're certain that you're uninjured."

Before Marcus had finished his sentence, Penn hauled Kaitlyn unceremoniously onto her feet, nudged Stephanie aside and ducked under the splintered bench to see what had broken loose. A minute later he pulled himself out with a grunt of disgust. "If the rest of this deck is built the same way," he warned, "I'd check on my insurance coverage if I were you, Stephanie."

There were tiny surprised shrieks and a rush of feet as most of the crowd deserted the deck. Penn looked startled. "I didn't say it wasn't safe," he called.

"It certainly sounded like it," Kaitlyn said grumpily. She gingerly started to dust off the seat of her shorts.

"Watch out; you've got splinters all over," Penn said. "Here, let me—"

She wheeled around. "Thanks anyway. I can take care of it."

He shrugged. "Suit yourself." He turned to the sole remaining woman on the deck, who was still sitting placidly in her lawn chair. "Too bad you didn't have your camera today, Jill," he said. "That would have made a great action sequence."

"It was a moment straight out of low-grade comic film," she agreed.

"Video would have been a nice touch. But I'd rather do stills, myself." He stretched out a hand to help her up.

Jill complained, "You're going to make me move? A woman in my condition? Surely it's safe here now that everyone else is off the deck."

"It's time to light the bonfire, anyway. When is the baby due?"

"About three weeks. And it's babies, by the way—plural."

Kaitlyn said, "You sound a lot calmer about it than when you first told me."

"Well, it's either two humans or one small hippopotamus, so if I have my choice—"

"That's our girl, always seeing the positive side of things." Kaitlyn tried to crane her neck far enough to see the back of her shorts. Were there really splinters?

Marcus was still fussing. "Are you certain you're not hurt?"

Penn didn't say a word, but the look he shot at Kaitlyn was incredulous—as if he didn't quite believe Marcus's concern could be real. It made her feel rather cross, and she said shortly, "I'm fine. Let's go down to the bonfire, all right?"

The sun had just dropped behind the wooded rim of the hills, and so the light that remained in the little valley was soft and pale and dappled by the long shadows of the trees.

Flames were already beginning to lick greedily at the kindling under the stack of driftwood. The adults settled themselves in chairs and on blankets, while the older children began to perform what they fondly thought was a war dance around the fire.

"Where did you guys find all the firewood, anyway?" someone called from across the circle. "Did you chop down Sentinel Oak?"

There was a chorus of chuckles and quick retorts.

"—the one landmark of Springhill?"

"And ruin all the fun our kids will have up there some-day?"

"*Our* kids? They'd never dare!"

"On second thought, cutting it down isn't a bad idea."

Marcus said calmly, "Sentinel Oak? I don't think I've heard about that."

Kaitlyn managed to suppress a groan. "Later," she said, under her breath.

Marcus frowned.

"It's a lovers' lane," Penn explained helpfully. He'd speared two hot dogs on a peeled sapling stick and was dangling them over the flames. "Hasn't Kaitlyn taken you up there yet? How long have you been in Springhill, anyway?" He didn't wait for an answer. "Just take the ring road around town and turn off at Blackberry Hill— What on earth is the matter with you, Kitten? That's a horrible noise you're making."

Kaitlyn jumped up and stalked off without a word.

"That sort of conduct is really quite unbecoming, Caldwell," she heard Marcus say as she left the circle of firelight. "As well as insulting to Kaitlyn, of course." It sounded like a warning.

There was a small, constricted silence, and then Penn said sadly, "You're quite right, Marcus. I just don't know what comes over me at moments like these."

She gritted her teeth and walked a little faster, her feet grinding into the sand. He doesn't know what comes over him, indeed! she thought. He's a troublemaker, that's what's wrong with him. He always has been one—doing things like talking me into wearing roller skates to the prom, and engineering the collapse of the homecoming queen's throne—just because he likes to see what will happen next. Damn him, why couldn't he just stay away from here?

She picked her way across a damp patch of sand and climbed onto a large, flat rock that overhung the edge of the water. She pulled her feet up and wrapped her arms around her knees, and listened to the water lapping against the shore beneath her.

"Don't get so upset," she told herself. He couldn't come between her and Marcus unless she let him; Marcus was annoyed with him, that was obvious, but he certainly wasn't taking Penn seriously. If she could just stay calm, in a few days Penn would be gone.

But in the meantime...

She heard his step on the sand, soft though it was. He had always moved like a wild creature through the twilight. She stayed very still on her rock, not even turning her head, hoping to somehow go unnoticed.

He climbed onto the rock beside her with a stalk of grass in his hand, and began thoughtfully chewing on it.

"You'll give yourself liver flukes." Kaitlyn didn't look at him. "I suppose you came after me to apologize?"

"Not at all. I wasn't doing anything to be ashamed of. I was just giving your Marcus a verbal tour of the highlights of Springhill, Kitten."

She said, between her teeth, "Dammit, Penn, would you stop calling me that?"

"Why? Because it reminds you of Sentinel Oak, and all the fun we used to have up there?"

His voice was cool, and she instantly regretted losing control of herself and letting him guess that it bothered her—not only the name, but the memories. "Not at all," she said firmly. "Because nothing ever happened at Sentinel Oak that was worth talking about."

"That's true. There were always too many people up there. Everything exciting happened right here at the lake, didn't it? Watching the moonlight on the water—and listening to the thunder in the hills—"

His hand came up to fling the stalk of grass out into the dark water, but instead of dropping back to his side, his fingertips came to rest on the curve of her cheek, turning her face to his.

There was one instant when she could have screamed, or pulled away from him and jumped from the rock. She could have unbalanced him with a shove. She could have—

But she didn't. Some nerve deep inside her seemed to have short-circuited and left her incapable of motion, or of feeling anything except the horrible fluttering at the base of her throat that kept her from drawing enough breath to protest.

Her lips felt stiff as cardboard under his gently questing mouth. It was like experiencing the very first kiss of her life all over again—with all the uncertainty, the hesitancy, the creeping fear that somehow she wasn't doing it quite right.

Then something changed, and her lips softened and warmed and seemed to melt against his. Penn made a little animal sound of satisfaction, and his hand slipped from her face to the nape of her neck, to pull her more closely against him and deepen the caress.

Some last fleeting instinct of self-preservation warned her, and she ducked away from that possessive hand. She rubbed the back of her fingers against her mouth, only half conscious of what she was doing.

"Trying to get rid of the taste of me?" he asked softly. "You can't do it that way, Kitten."

"Don't bet on it," she said fiercely. "Just leave me alone, Penn. Go away." She jumped from the rock to the beach, landing awkwardly with a jolt to her ankle. But she swallowed her gasp—it was mostly fear, anyway, not pain—and started back up the beach to the safety of the firelight.

The party had shattered into small knots of people spread across the beach, some still at the fire, others at the picnic tables or relaxing under the trees, and she passed a half-dozen groups in her search for Marcus.

When she spotted him, she dropped to the sand beside him with a sigh of relief, before she had a chance to think about how strange her haste would look—or to wonder if there was some obvious sign she should have wiped away. There was no need to worry about smeared lipstick, for she wasn't wearing any. But what if the hint of Penn's after-shave was clinging to her now?

Marcus turned to her. "You're all right, darling?"

But there was nothing more than affectionate concern in his voice, and her heart gradually slowed from pounding panic to normal. She squeezed his arm and leaned her head against his shoulder. "I'm fine."

"It's a beautiful night. I see now why you like the lake so much."

He trusts me, Kaitlyn thought. *He loves me. He likes the things I like. He's solid and reliable. How could I ever have doubted my feelings for him?*

"I thought you would. I'm glad." And then she leaned a littler closer, and murmured, "Perhaps we can have a cabin here someday, darling—when we're married?"

CHAPTER THREE

SHE OVERSLEPT the next morning, and was jolted awake by a thump in the attic directly above her bedroom. "Great," she muttered. "I'm glad that Mother is developing some enthusiasm for this move. But why at this unholy hour?" Then she looked at the clock on the night table and climbed out of bed. It wasn't all that early, after all, and there were those tuxedos to check on. And the florist wanted her opinion on how he should anchor the bouquets that Sabrina wanted to float in the Harts' swimming pool. . . .

A bright-eyed little dog climbed out of his basket in the corner of the kitchen and pranced across to greet her, yipping happily as if seeing her was a once-in-a-lifetime surprise.

Kaitlyn was not flattered. "Schnoodle, please," she said wearily. "Mother will hear you and come down, and you know I can't talk sensibly till I've had some caffeine." She patted the dog until he calmed down, then put him out into the garden, and as soon as the coffee maker had finished its cycle she poured herself a cup and went out into the sunshine herself.

Schnoodle looked up hopefully when she appeared, but when he saw that she wasn't carrying any promising plates or baskets or platters—only a notepad and pen and a calendar—he went back to snuffling along the edges of the flower beds.

The air was already warm, threatening a breathlessly hot day, but the flagstone patio was still pleasantly cool under her bare feet. Kaitlyn sat down at the glass-topped table with her cup cradled in one hand and the blank notebook before her and began to tear off sheets of paper to make lists. "Things to do today," she muttered. "Things to box up for my apartment. Things to buy so we can pack everything else—" She paged through her calendar and sighed. There wasn't a blank day in the next two weeks, even before she penciled in time for apartment hunting and packing. Why couldn't this move have waited till next month when no one seemed to require her services?

The garden gate creaked, not its usual single rasping protest but a repeated, rhythmic pattern. Kaitlyn leaned around an azalea bush and said, "Must you encourage that thing to make noise?"

Penn didn't look up. He was exercising the gate, inspecting the hinges. "It could be fixed, you know."

At the sound of his voice, Schnoodle's nose came up out of a patch of periwinkle and began to twitch excitedly. The twitch grew into a shudder that racked him from ears to tail, and the shudder was followed by a peal of shrill, yapping barks that had roughly the same impact on Kaitlyn as fingernails scraping on a blackboard.

"Schnoodle!" she said sharply, "cut that out before you wake the neighbors!"

The gate stopped creaking, and Penn said, almost at her elbow, "Schnoodle, old fella—do you remember me?" He stooped to scratch the dog's ears, and Schnoodle abased himself on the flagstone path, wriggling and panting and grinning as only a mixed-breed schnauzer could.

There had never been anything Schnoodle wouldn't do, if it would win Penn's attention for him, Kaitlyn thought. Some creatures had no pride at all....

Penn stopped scratching the dog and straightened up. He looked taller than ever today, she thought, but that might only be because his cutoff jeans and half-buttoned shirt left so much more of him visible this morning. Even his chest was tanned under the curls of dark hair. And his knees were nicely browned, too. How had he managed that, she wondered. Working as a lifeguard?

"So? Do you want me to fix it?"

Kaitlyn shrugged. "The gate? Don't bother. Let the new owners worry about it." If she had hoped to surprise him, she was mistaken.

"Yes, I heard the house sold. I don't understand how the newspaper makes any money in this town," he added thoughtfully. "Nobody needs to read it. It's funny, though, how no one told me about your engagement till last night. I'd have expected to hear that the minute I hit town." He looked innocently inquisitive, as if he seriously expected an answer.

Kaitlyn sipped her coffee and turned back to her lists. Masking tape, string, marking pens... "Amazing, isn't it, how gossip works?" she said sweetly.

"I suppose I really should apologize to Marcus for trespassing on his territory last night." He pulled a chair around and sprawled in it.

"Please don't bother."

"Oh? Why not? Don't you want him to hear about that kiss?"

Kaitlyn shrugged. "It was certainly nothing worth talking about."

Penn tipped his chair back on two legs and murmured, "How long have you been engaged, anyway? I thought, myself, that Marcus looked a little stunned last night, as if the whole idea was news to him. I've got it! You proposed to him instead of the other way around, didn't you?"

The back screen door slammed, and Audrey appeared. "Look what I found, Kaitlyn— Oh, hello, Penn! It's your blanket, darling, the one you wouldn't go to sleep without when you were little."

Kaitlyn looked at the scrap of worn, grayish flannel with distaste. "Throw it away," she recommended.

"No, dear. You'll feel differently about it when you have children of your own, and they have blankets. I'll put it in the box with your baby gowns."

Kaitlyn sighed. "Is that what you've been doing this morning, Mother? Preserving my baby clothes?" Left to herself, she thought, it would take her mother years to clean out the house.

"No, I was looking for my wedding dress, actually. Not that I expect you'll want to wear it, Kaitlyn, but I was just feeling a little sentimental after you and Marcus told me your news last night."

Penn's grin lighted his face and danced in his eyes, and Kaitlyn thought about breaking her coffee cup over his head in retaliation.

"That changes your plans, doesn't it, Audrey?" he observed. "I suppose you'll be looking for a even smaller place, since Kaitlyn will be moving in with Marcus."

Audrey looked startled. "Oh, she wouldn't do that before the wedding—" She stopped, and finally added, uncertainly, "Would you, dear?"

"My mistake," Penn said smoothly. "Of course she wouldn't. And it's going to be a big wedding, I'm sure. When will it be?"

"We haven't talked about it," Kaitlyn said reluctantly.

"Amazing. I'd have thought that would be the first thing to discuss. After an engagement ring, of course," he added, with a meaningful glance at her bare left hand.

Her fingers clenched hard on the handle of her cup.

Penn eyed her white knuckles and said, "Well, I must be running along. Actually I just stopped by to tell you if there is anything I can do to help with your move, Audrey, please let me know. That gate, for instance—"

"Oh, can you stop that horrible creaking, Penn?" Audrey sounded almost worshipful. "It's so difficult these days to get a handyman for little jobs like that, but it annoys me so."

"It will only annoy you for thirteen more days, Mother," Kaitlyn said under her breath, but it was too late. Audrey followed Penn to the gate, saying something about the downspouts, and the two of them disappeared around the front of the house, leaving the gate swinging and creaking.

At Kaitlyn's feet, Schnoodle whimpered a little and looked around nearsightedly.

"Serves you right," she told the dog unsympathetically, and got up to close the gate. "You shouldn't have assumed he'd stick around forever." She looked unseeingly across the brilliant beds of daisies and the heavy masses of blooms on the climbing roses. "Nobody should ever depend on Penn," she said to herself. "Life is much easier that way—without expectations."

SHE RAN INTO HIM AGAIN that afternoon at Springhill Hardware. She never would have gotten into the checkout line behind him if she'd seen him first. However, she wasn't looking at the other customers; she was trying to review her list while balancing half a dozen rolls of packing tape and the dispenser to apply it, a carton of assorted labels, a ball of twine and two pairs of scissors. Once in line, she could hardly turn around and fade back into the aisles; it would have looked suspicious. So she stood there with her arms loaded and watched while he reopened the long-dormant Caldwell charge account.

"Pretty heavy-duty tools to fix one small gate," she observed as the clerk was writing up his purchases. "I can understand the hammer, but do you really need a wrecking bar to take the hinges off?"

Penn signed his bill with a flourish. "This isn't for the gate. The cabin needs a bit of work before I can be comfortable there."

"The cabin needs—you mean you're going to *stay?*"

His eyebrows went up slightly. "You sound amazed," he said. "No, it's even more than amazement. You sound seriously offended at the idea that I'm going to be around for a while. Now why... ?"

"Never mind what I think," Kaitlyn said hastily. A while? That could be anything from a couple of weeks to the summer—certainly no longer, if he was staying in the cabin. "The truth is, you're between jobs at the moment, right?"

Penn smiled. "You're too fast for me, darling," he murmured.

"Were you fired this time, or did you just walk away?"

"Oh, I walked away," he said airily. "That looks so much better on my résumé than being bounced off the job. Besides, job or no job, I wouldn't miss your wedding for the world. So I thought I'd better stay right here so you'd know where to send the invitation."

"I'll keep it in mind," she muttered and dropped her pile of purchases next to the cash register. A roll of tape fell off and rolled halfway to the door; Penn retrieved it and leaned against the counter to watch.

"I'll bet it will be a real exhibition." He must have seen the sparks flare in her eyes, for he added smoothly, "I mean, of course, that you must be planning to have all the frills, just to show your clients everything that's available."

She had to bite her tongue, but she managed not to answer.

"Come to think of it, you might not need invitations," Penn mused. "You could just put advertisements in the newspaper. You could turn the whole thing into a sort of demonstration bridal fair, and deduct the entire cost from your income tax next year."

She swallowed hard, and forced herself to smile. "Thank you very much for your advice, Penn, but—"

"I won't even send you a bill for the consultation." He held the door for her and appealed to a young man with a shaggy mustache who was just coming in. "Stan, that's right, isn't it? If someone in Kaitlyn's position throws a sample wedding and invites all her prospective clients, it's a legitimate business expense, correct?"

"Why ask me?" the young man said with a shrug. "I don't specialize in tax law. But as long as we're talking of prospective clients, do you have a business card, Kaitlyn? The wedding won't be till next year, but—"

Penn looked shocked. "You too?" he groaned. "Is there a damned virus in the water supply around here?"

Kaitlyn rummaged in her bag and handed the young man her card with a smile. "Give my best wishes to Elaine," she said softly, and then, because Stan was looking very pink all of a sudden, she put a card into Penn's hand, as well. "Just in case the virus catches up with you, too."

"Thank you," Penn said politely. "I'll put it with my collection of oddities from around the world." He glanced at the card as they walked across the parking lot. "Kaitlyn Ross, Wedding Consultant. Is that all? Oh, it's elegant all right, with the copperplate script, but how very dull."

"Reliable," Kaitlyn snapped. "Conservative. Solid. *Not* dull."

"I'm disappointed. Here I thought you'd have called your business something cute—something original. It's not too late to change, you know. I've got the perfect name— The Bridal Path. And your slogan could be something like, 'Now you no longer have to trot down the long road to a blissful wedding by yourself.'"

"Penn, that's the worst... Please don't tell me you've been in advertising, too."

"All right," Penn said happily. "I won't."

She threw her bag into the back of her car with unnecessary force. It was foolish to trade gibes with a man who had nothing better to do than think up new ones.

She wondered if he ever got tired of living that way.

SABRINA CAUGHT UP WITH her in the ladies' room at the country club that night. "You have to do something," she announced. "Karl is determined that he's going to have Penn Caldwell as his best man, and I swear to heaven if he does—"

"He won't," Kaitlyn told her soothingly. "Karl's not crazy, and he's not a gambler; he knows the kind of strange notion that is apt to flit into Penn's head at the last instant. The odds are he'd decide to take off for Tahiti or Botswana, with your wedding ring still in his pocket."

Sabrina screeched, "And that thought is supposed to comfort me?"

"Don't worry. It's too late to order another tuxedo from the rental place. I made sure of that today, so if Karl makes any more noise about it, tell him to call me."

She was still shaking her head over the incident when she got back to the dining room. How Karl and Sabrina were going to work out real issues when they couldn't agree on a best man— Oh, well, she reminded herself, I don't have to guarantee the success of the marriage, only the wedding day!

A couple of minutes later Marcus asked what on earth she was brooding about. "You haven't heard a thing I've said," he accused.

"I'm sorry. It's just that I think this next wedding is going to be the death of me yet. I'm learning the hard way that a wedding that's twice the size of the usual one doesn't present double the problems—it's more like a multiple of ten." She fidgeted with her dinner fork. "And when the bride and groom start fighting, too, things get impossible. It's a shame all my clients can't be like Laura McCarthy; she's a doll. Oh, I forgot to tell you the latest! Stan Spaulding and Elaine—"

"Another wedding?" Marcus's tone was notably lacking in enthusiasm.

"Not till next year sometime."

Marcus sighed and reached for the wine bottle to refill her glass. "Perhaps you shouldn't book things so far ahead, Kaitlyn."

She stared at him in stupefaction. "How else could I run the sort of business I'm in? It takes the better part of a year to plan and arrange a big wedding."

"I know it does. But I've been giving the matter a lot of thought. Are you certain you're going to want to continue your business after we're married?"

"Yes." Her voice was cool and firm. "Why on earth do you ask?"

"Because you must admit it's a problem, darling. Whenever we have a chance to be together, you're tied up with a wedding."

"On the weekends, yes. The rest of the time, you're tied up with your business," she pointed out.

"Kaitlyn, be reasonable."

"I *am* being reasonable. I agree there's a problem. But who says we have to be together on weekends? Can't you adjust your schedule sometimes? I'm nearly always free in the mornings."

His voice went up slightly with annoyance. "I can't very well entertain clients to dinner at nine in the morning, can I?"

"Oh—so we're not really talking just about time together, but your obligations, and how I fit into them?"

"You know it's more than that. But as far as entertaining my clients, that's an important part of my job, and I'd like to have you share in that when we're married." He reached across the table for her hand. "I'd like to have you use that unique flair of yours for me, too—to arrange parties and make sure people have fun. Isn't that part of what being married is, Kaitlyn? Sharing things like that?"

She couldn't disagree with him. Not exactly. She wanted to support his career and be a valuable part of it. And she certainly didn't want to quarrel about it; they were hardly even engaged, and already they were fighting. "Of course, Marcus." Her voice was subdued. "But the subject came up rather suddenly, that's all. I love my job, and the idea of giving it up completely, coming out of the blue like that..."

"You're barely breaking even," Marcus said coolly.

"But I'm not doing it for the money. As long as I can support myself—which I'm doing, by the way—"

He smiled and squeezed her hand. "But you won't have to support yourself for long." He fumbled in his pocket and pulled out a tiny velvet-covered box. "I wanted to give you this before I left." He flicked the tiny latch on the box and lifted the lid.

The ring inside was a wide gold band, with a gigantic marquise diamond surrounded by tiny rubies. Her gaze lifted to meet his eyes. "Before you leave? Where are you going?"

"Louisiana—a business trip." He took the ring from the box and slid it onto her finger. "I'll see you Friday evening when I get home. We can have dinner and talk over our own wedding plans for a change."

She shook her head. "Friday is Sabrina's rehearsal."

And with the wedding on Saturday night, she remembered, she wouldn't have a free minute that day, either.

Marcus sighed. "Sunday, then," he said firmly. "I'll be bringing a couple of the corporation's executives back with me. We can play golf."

Sunday would be nearly as bad, she reflected, with all the cleanup to be done after the extravaganza of the wedding. But she nodded. She'd fit it all in somehow.

Marcus was right, she thought. Their schedules did collide, regularly, and it wasn't going to get any better. Or any worse, either, she supposed, but now it was going to be more obvious, because they would want to spend all their time together. He was right—something would have to give.

EVEN THE WEATHERMAN smiled on Sabrina Hart's wedding day; in early June, Springhill could be miserably humid and sticky, but this Saturday was flawless. The late-afternoon sun was shining, but it wasn't beating down on the concrete and imported tile that surrounded the Harts'

backyard pool. There was a gentle breeze, just enough to
stir the leaves of the tulip trees, but not enough to tug at
the centerpieces already in place on the pool-side tables or
threaten to tip over the huge bouquets that were now
floating placidly in the water. There had been enough rain
so that the lawn was lush and green, but not so much that
the flowers in the brilliant borders had been beaten down.
In short, if Kaitlyn had picked out each condition from
some mail-order catalog and assembled the day herself, it
could not have been more perfect.

Inside, the caterer's men were putting the last of the
bridal cakes into place on the huge banquet table, atop a
cloud of pale yellow chiffon. Kaitlyn hovered nearby,
breath held, until the cake was safely balanced on its foot-
tall pillars. Then she relaxed a little, but she stayed to
watch as yards of yellow ribbon and lace were draped and
twisted gently into place to coordinate the multitude of
small cakes, each a different flavor, into one huge spun-
sugar sculpture, topped with fresh flowers. The caterer
gave a final nod to the finished result, and one of his as-
sistants flipped a switch to illuminate the hundreds of tiny
twinkling lights that had been wound through the chiffon
cloud and between the cakes. The cake looked like a fairy
confection—as if it was floating in the stars.

Kaitlyn gave a thumbs-up signal to the caterer and ran
a practiced eye over the rest of the huge living room. A
portable bar had been set up at each end, already well
stocked. The food? Well, she'd simply have to have faith
on that question; it would arrive while they were all at the
church.

There was nothing more to be done here now. She
checked her tiny wristwatch and started back through the
house to make sure Sabrina and all her bridesmaids were
dressed on schedule.

Giggles greeted her in the bedroom wing, which seemed to be full of girls rustling around in full-skirted buttercup-yellow gowns. In front of the huge triple mirror in the master bedroom Sabrina stood in her white satin gown, cut so low that it barely clung to her shoulders, clasping a cascade of white orchids while Jill struggled to get the train to lie just right across the carpet.

Kaitlyn suffered one sharp pang of panic. What was Jill doing here? Then she forced herself to relax. "I thought your partner was doing the pictures today," she said.

Jill gave her an absentminded half smile and turned to pick up her camera. "We were both going to work this one. But his daughter was in a car accident this morning."

"Is she all right?"

"She'll be fine, but he was pretty shaken up, and of course he wanted to be with her. Look down at your flowers, Sabrina. That's right—now a soft romantic smile."

It looked more like a pout to Kaitlyn. She decided to ignore the unexpected change of photographers; there was nothing that could be done about it now, anyway. Sabrina's pictures would certainly not suffer.

She took a deep breath and forced herself to relax. From this moment on, until late tonight when the last guest left, there would not be an instant to let down her guard. Fortunately, Kaitlyn told herself, she thrived on this kind of stress.

"The limousines will be here in half an hour," she said. "Everybody ready? Any loose buttons or slipping zippers? Let's get them fixed now. Don't forget your hair spray and lipstick, girls—"

She cajoled them into the cars and off to the church, and she pushed the speed limit herself in order to have a little extra time to check the details in the sanctuary before the slower-paced limousines arrived. It was a larger church than any she had worked in before, and it was even more difficult to make sure that each blossom and candle and ribbon was in place while still staying out of sight herself.

The carillon struck the hour, and the familiar expectant hush fell over the church as Kaitlyn made her way down the side aisle. This time it was Penn who gave her a thumbs-up sign from the congregation—Penn, sitting beside Audrey Ross, and wearing a dark gray summer suit, not the white tie and tails that the ushers were garbed in. Kaitlyn breathed a little easier at the sight. She hadn't quite been able to shake the notion that despite the agreement she'd reached with Karl to leave Penn out of things, they might pull a substitution at the last minute.

The bride's limousine was just pulling up. Jill was waiting at the door, camera in hand, and Sabrina's mother was hovering in the foyer. "You're late," she accused. "The whole wedding is late."

"The bells are just finishing," Kaitlyn said calmly. "Sabrina's beautiful music would get lost in all that clamor if it tried to compete, don't you think?" She summoned an usher. "Now don't worry about another thing, Mrs. Hart. I promise it will all go smoothly."

Mrs. Hart did not seem comforted by the reassurance, but she went off down the aisle. Kaitlyn smiled. The mother of the bride was practically guaranteed to have a nervous spasm or to lose her temper in the last minutes before the ceremony. Sometimes Kaitlyn made bets with herself as to which it would be—and she'd been right this time.

Sabrina came up the stairs on her father's arm.

"Right on time," Kaitlyn said, and when the photographer did nothing, she added, "Jill?"

Jill jumped. "Sorry, Kaitlyn. I'm moving a bit slower than usual today."

"I'm not surprised. You look awfully tired, trying to do it all—" Then she saw fleeting pain cross Jill's face, and she added, with horrible certainty, "Except it's more than just being tired, isn't it? Oh Lord, Jill, you're in labor, aren't you?"

Jill struggled to smile. "Of course not. The babies aren't due for two weeks."

"Twins?" the matron of honor asked, with almost-ghoulish cheerfulness. "Don't twins always come early?"

"They'd better not appear on my wedding day," Sabrina said through clenched teeth.

Her father cleared his throat. "What day it is doesn't make much difference to babies, Sabrina. If it was me, Miss Ross, I'd get her to the hospital right away."

Kaitlyn looked at him in astonishment; she'd almost forgotten he was there. As a matter of fact, those were the first words she could recall him saying through the whole long year of planning this wedding.

Jill shook her head. "Let's just get the wedding under way. I can't leave you in the lurch, and—"

This time the pain was obviously worse. A fine mist of perspiration appeared on Jill's lovely face, and she didn't object when Mr. Hart eased her into a nearby chair.

Kaitlyn's head felt like a kettle drum. "Yes, you can! As soon as I find your husband you're going to the hospital. Now give me that camera," she ordered. "I'll take the damned pictures myself if I have to." *And I may have to,* she thought grimly. With Jill's partner tending to his injured daughter, and no other professional studio in Springhill, and a wedding ready to start . . .

Sabrina's eyes were wide with shock, as if to say that this could not be happening to her.

The church was totally silent when Kaitlyn went in. The last softly played love song had ended, the organist was waiting for her cue to start the wedding march and the expectant hush of a few minutes before was mutating into an anxious stillness.

Kaitlyn could almost hear the congregation wondering what was wrong. Had the bride not arrived, after all? Had the groom walked out? Had someone—oh, what a deliciously scandalous idea!—come forward with a reason why these two should not be wed?

From the front pew Sabrina's mother was staring at the altar, eyes narrowed with suspicion. The blithe reassurance Kaitlyn had given the woman just a few minutes ago tasted bitter in her mouth now. *"I promise it will all go smoothly."*

That promise was why people hired a wedding consultant in the first place, she reminded herself. If she didn't deliver on it, she could kiss any future recommendations goodbye. That in itself would be bad enough, but she couldn't picture Mrs. Hart simply being silent, either; the woman would no doubt tell everyone who would listen exactly what her opinion was of Kaitlyn Ross. Business would certainly go downhill—and Marcus might get his wish, after all.

At least she would have a good excuse for quitting, she told herself in a feeble attempt to be positive. If she said she was giving it up because Marcus didn't want her to work, it wouldn't look as if she'd been run out of business.

She found Jill's husband and sent him out to the anteroom, then let her gaze rove over the congregation, trying to remember who might be enough of a camera buff to take over Jill's complicated equipment now. There must be someone here who could fill in. There was always one in every crowd who insisted on having a picture of everything. There had to be someone who had experience beyond vacation snapshots....

She remembered a snippet of conversation—one she had paid little attention to at the time—and turned purposefully toward the groom's side of the church. Penn looked startled when she dropped into the seat beside him and demanded, without preface, "I need a favor."

"I'm listening."

"I've absolutely got to have someone who knows cameras. Right now."

He glanced around the church. "It's a bit late to be hiring, don't you think?"

She gritted her teeth. "Babies and car crashes are acts of God, Penn, not my fault."

"What makes you think I could step in?"

"You used to play around with a camera, and you were talking to Jill last Sunday as if you still knew a little about it. And didn't you say you've been doing picture postcards?"

"That was for fun. I'm not exactly professional—not at the sort of thing you've got in mind."

"Have you got any better ideas?"

He was silent.

"I'll tell you what to shoot, for heaven's sake!" She put a hand on his sleeve; her nails tapped anxiously against the gray linen. "Look, Penn, I'll kneel and beg if you want. I need you desperately—"

"Why, Kaitlyn—" His palm came down softly over the back of her hand.

The warm pressure had a certain comforting appeal. She finished recklessly, "You can name your price."

Penn smiled. "Now that's an offer I can't refuse," he murmured. "I'll have to carefully consider my fees, of course, since I've never done this before. Is it all right if I let you know after the wedding's over?''

"Dammit, Penn—"

His eyebrows went up slightly.

The silence in the church had given way to whispers and murmurs and buzzes of speculation, and the bride's mother was sitting rigidly in the front pew, her chin up in a challenge that didn't bode well for anyone who crossed her. Compared to the prospect of facing Mrs. Hart, Kaitlyn thought, a little financial blackmail from Penn was hardly even a threat.

Kaitlyn sighed. "Absolutely," she said with resignation. "Think it over and give me your price. In the meantime, can we go to work?"

CHAPTER FOUR

FOR KAITLYN, the entire wedding ceremony was no more than a blur; she heard hardly a word of it. She moved mechanically around the church, trying to direct Penn but ending up simply following at his heels. After the first five minutes of hissing orders—orders he seemed not to hear—Kaitlyn gave up and sat in a back corner of the church and tried to keep from chewing all her nails down to the quick. He seemed to know what he was doing, she told herself. At least he hadn't dropped the camera yet, and he hadn't fallen over the balcony rail.

The final chords of the recessional were still ringing out when the newly married couple paused at the back of the church for a kiss to be immortalized on film. Then Karl said, "What the hell happened to hold everything up? And why are you running around here with a camera, Penn?"

Sabrina, reminded of the change of plans, stopped smiling and glared at Penn. "This had better work out," she said ominously.

He shrugged. "Just don't try to hold me responsible if you frown and break the camera."

Kaitlyn couldn't help wondering if that was a threat to sabotage the pictures. She started to protest, until from the corner of her eyes she saw Mrs. Hart bearing down on her. She promptly stopped worring about Penn and said, "Quick! Into the limousine, or your guests will want to gather right here and congratulate you, and you'll never get to the reception.''

Karl didn't even look around; he carefully tucked his bride into the limousine. Kaitlyn almost pushed Penn toward her car, which was parked in a reserved spot nearby so she could get out with no difficulty. He took one look at her face and said, ''If you don't mind, I'll drive. It wouldn't be appropriate to have you squealing tires in front of a church.'' He took the keys out of her hand.

She didn't argue about it; with the level of concentration she was capable of at the moment, if she was driving they'd probably end up in Arkansas.

Come to think of it, she reflected, that wasn't such a bad idea. Anywhere but Springhill.

''I hate to mention it, but haven't we missed something?'' Penn asked. ''Such as the formal family photos at the church?''

Kaitlyn shook her head. She eyed the leather camera bag he'd shoved into the seat between them, and then let her head fall back against the velvet upholstery with a sigh. ''Sabrina's mother thinks they're stiff and nasty, so you're just to shoot a few groups at the reception.''

''What a shame. That means I can't in good conscience charge you as much as I otherwise would.''

Kaitlyn sat up slowly. ''If you had any conscience at all, Penn, you'd do it as your wedding gift.''

He smiled, and his dark eyes danced with silvery lights. ''Trying to change the rules, Kitten? I thought you said I could name my price.''

A traffic light glared red, and he brought the car to a smooth stop. Kaitlyn tapped her fingers nervously on the upholstery, and Penn reached for her hand. ''I see you finally got your engagement ring.''

His fingers were warm, and he took an uncomfortably long time studying the ring, turning it to watch the long rays of evening sunlight splinter through the depths of the diamond.

"The traffic light has changed," she pointed out.

"So what? The limousine's behind us." But Penn put her hand down and turned his attention back to the street. "That's quite a rock," he said, a block or so later. "It's a little on the yellowish side to be perfect, perhaps, but—"

"Don't tell me. You've graded diamonds in Amsterdam, too."

He shook his head. "Not yet. It wouldn't be a bad job, though."

In the Harts' driveway, he left the engine running and grabbed for the camera bag as the limousine pulled up behind them. Kaitlyn sighed, slid across into the driver's seat, and moved the car to the back of the house. At least there was one advantage in hanging around with Penn, she thought. For a full minute there, she'd forgotten all about her anxiety over the photographs, in the urge to hit him over the head with whatever large and heavy object came to hand.

The reception was no improvement. In the midst of the champagne toasts, Penn told her, with the air of a man who has just hit the jackpot, "I've got it! The only reason for bridesmaids at these affairs is to dress them up like dumplings so the bride will look lovely by comparison. Right?"

"Dammit, Penn—" Then she swallowed hard, and forced herself to smile. There was no advantage in getting into an argument with the man over a half dozen buttercup-yellow dresses. He was right, as a matter of fact; two of Sabrina's bridesmaids did look like dumplings.

And a bit later, when the orchestra began to play at the poolside and Marcus asked her to dance, Penn looked stricken. But he said bravely, "Go ahead, Kitten. Have a little fun. I think I can handle the overwhelming responsibility by myself for a while."

Marcus saw the frustration in her eyes as she surveyed the two of them. "Never mind," he said crisply, and moved off toward the bar.

Kaitlyn wheeled around, hands planted on hips. "Dammit, Penn—"

"Kitten, I'm beginning to think that's my name. All three syllables of it."

"—it's not unreasonable for Marcus to want to dance with me at a party!"

"That's true. Does he always head for a drink when he's disappointed? I'd be worried about that, if I were you." He didn't wait for an answer, but moved off capably to capture a few more images of the dancing crowd.

"You're no help," Kaitlyn muttered.

Mrs. Hart appeared beside her. Her smile was sweet, but her voice cut like a razor. "That's precisely what I was thinking about you, Miss Ross. I'm sure you understand why I won't be paying the rest of your fee until after we've seen the photographs."

Kaitlyn shrugged miserably, but she couldn't blame the woman for being unhappy. A year's planning and thousands of dollars spent to make a perfect wedding— and sheer bad luck at the end. No wonder Mrs. Hart was looking for someone to blame. She shivered and went to check on the dinner service.

The evening dragged more than any other she had ever experienced, but finally it was all over. The last champagne toast had been drunk, and the newly married couple were ferried off in the long white limousine, and the guests drifted away. "You can go now, Penn," Kaitlyn told him. "Just leave the film and the cameras with me, and I'll get them back to Jill."

"I can't. Remember? You practically kidnapped me from the church and dragged me out here in the wilds, far from anywhere, so now it's up to you to take care of me." He gave her a cheerful grin and snagged the last boiled shrimp from a tray that the caterer was removing. "I've been debating the pay scale for my work tonight, by the way."

That sounded like trouble, and Kaitlyn tried to forestall it. "If you don't know what to charge, I'll check it out with Jill and pay you the usual rates."

"What happened to naming my own price?"

Kaitlyn watched a guest who was sagging against the now-closed bar and wondered if it was going to be necessary to remove him. "What about doing it for the love of your friends?"

"I'm not sure exactly what you have in mind, but it sounds as if it could be intriguing," he admitted.

"I meant your friendship with Karl," she said, a little more sharply than she'd intended.

Penn's eyebrows rose. "And leave you out of it altogether? Oh, I couldn't do that, Kitten. Don't worry; I'll let you know as soon as I come up with an idea."

"I'll be holding my breath," Kaitlyn muttered.

"Really? Don't let Marcus see you doing it—he might wonder if we're up to something kinky. He's watching us intently from the corner, by the way, like a jealous husband." He swiped a couple of Swedish meatballs from the hors d'oeuvre bar and smiled at her as warmly as if she'd just uttered the most tantalizing remark ever spoken. "Where are you going on your honeymoon?"

"I haven't the vaguest idea."

"Oh? You mean you're actually leaving that part to Marcus? Perhaps I should give him some suggestions."

"The Sahara Desert, I suppose," Kaitlyn said, remembering what she'd overheard him recommend to Karl.

He sounded shocked. "Of course not, Kitten. For you and Marcus, it will have to be something *really* special."

KAITLYN WAS TIRED ENOUGH to sleep around the clock, and she might have done so if it hadn't been for a persistent dream in which bits of photographic paper bearing brightly colored images of a headless bride and groom swirled about her face like hornets. The attack jolted her awake, and she found herself cowering in the middle of her bed, her arms raised protectively. She crawled out from the tangled sheets. It might be scarcely seven o'clock on a Sunday morning, but there was no sense in trying to go back to sleep after that.

She put Schnoodle out into the garden and made herself a pot of coffee. She was sitting on the terrace with her head in her hands, trying to figure out how long it would be before she knew for sure whether they had managed to salvage anything from last night's fiasco, when she heard a cheerful whistle coming around the corner of the house. Even if she hadn't recognized it, one look at Schnoodle, turning tight ecstatic circles in the middle of Audrey's favorite flower bed would have been enough to identify the whistler. She groaned.

Penn said unsympathetically, "You look as if you could use a good headache remedy." He put a tool kit down in the path just inside the garden gate and bent over to pet the dog.

"I certainly could, now that you're here," she muttered. "It's too early to fix the gate, you know. You'll wake the neighbors."

He pulled a chair around and straddled it. Schnoodle draped himself over Penn's foot and started happily licking his bare ankle. "That was good champagne last night," Penn said, "but no matter what the vintage, if you drink too much of it—"

"I am not suffering from an overdose of champagne. I never drink alcohol while I'm managing a party." She sat up. "And you're the one who's responsible for this, anyway—I've been having nightmares about your pictures."

"Is that all the thanks I get for helping you out of a jam? Is there any more coffee?"

"Why?"

"If you're not going to let me work, at least let me drink coffee."

"Why would you want to work? It's barely dawn."

"I've gotten used to keeping early hours."

"Oh? Why? Have you been in some Third World country that doesn't have electric lights yet? The coffee's in the kitchen."

He peeled the dog off his foot and vanished through the back door. Schnoodle flopped down beside the empty chair, looking glum.

The instant Penn returned with a mug in one hand and the coffeepot in the other, Kaitlyn said, "You see, I keep having this awful suspicion that you may have aimed the camera wrong and only got the bodies."

Penn filled his mug, inhaled the fragrance of coffee and sighed with satisfaction. "Now why would I do something like that?"

"Because for all I know, you're more experienced with a submachine gun than a camera these days."

Penn shook his head. "No, no. I just meant that Sabrina doesn't have such a great body. She's far too skinny, so of course I wouldn't—" He stopped with his cup raised almost to his lips and looked at her with concern. "You're a terrible example for Schnoodle, Kitten. Does Marcus know you growl in the mornings?"

"I only do it when I have to deal with you."

"In that case, I won't warn him. I don't see why you're so worried, though. However good those pictures look, they're doomed to end up in bits on Sabrina's living room floor someday."

"You don't think that marriage will last?"

"It sounds to me as if she got so caught up in planning the wedding that the marriage didn't matter anymore."

"That's a twist," Kaitlyn mused. "Penn Caldwell sounding almost like a romantic. It's true there's often a letdown after all the excitement is over, but that doesn't—"

Penn shook his head. "Karl and Sabrina are in for more than just a letdown. But we're not responsible for the whole marriage, thank heaven—only the pictures. Your contract does cover things like this, doesn't it? I mean, if a tornado takes the roof off a church just as the bride starts down the aisle, it's certainly not your fault, so—"

She shuddered. "Penn, please don't. I've got another wedding next weekend, and it's the height of tornado season."

"Sorry." He didn't sound it.

"Anyway, I like my job. Most of the time, at least. Not every bride is like Sabrina, not every mother is like hers and not every wedding is like yesterday's."

"Just the big ones."

"They tend to be more troublesome, yes. They also pay well."

He refilled his cup and leaned back in his chair. "So are you going to hire a coordinator for your big splash, or take care of all the arrangements yourself?"

"I'll do it myself. There really isn't anyone else I could trust, and I'd probably end up doing all the work, anyway."

He shrugged. "I was just wondering how you'll handle the actual wedding day. Surely you can't be running about like a sergeant-major in a Gilbert and Sullivan production and still have time to think about the vows, Kitten."

"If you're implying that I should be having second thoughts about marrying Marcus—"

Penn looked shocked. "Heaven forbid! That never even crossed my mind."

"Well, you can relax. I won't need to give my vows a lot of thought that day, because I know exactly what I'm doing. He's a wonderful man and—"

"And you love him very much," Penn said piously, over the rim of his cup.

Kaitlyn felt a brief and completely unreasonable urge to shove both the cup and his almost-sincere look down his throat. Then she remembered that nothing required her to sit there and listen to him, and she pushed her chair away and gathered her mug and the coffeepot into one hand. "I'm going back to bed," she said and started for the door. "Have fun fixing the gate."

"You're going to sleep through the best part of the day?" Penn scoffed. "Oh, you mean that you're still worn out from yesterday's excitement?" He shook his head sadly. "Perhaps someone should warn Marcus."

She bit her tongue, but it didn't help; she turned back to look at him, and the words seemed to tumble out unbidden. "Warn him? Why?"

Penn smiled. "Because if yesterday left you exhausted, what will your own big bash do? Kitten, darling, after getting through a day like the one you must be planning, you certainly aren't going to have enough energy left for the wedding night." He actually smiled as he said it. "Poor Marcus."

This time she made it inside the house. And she let the screen door bang, heedless of the neighbors. It made her feel a little better.

SHE WAS TERRIBLE on the golf course that afternoon; her nerves were frazzled and her coordination was shot, and on the tenth hole she picked up her ball and declared that she'd just ride the rest of the way. It didn't help that Marcus's business associates—two senior executives from TurfMaster's parent company—were treating her like the proverbial little woman, talking over her head as if she wasn't bright enough to know the fairway from the green. By the time they'd finished eighteen holes she was relieved just to be off the course and back in the clubhouse.

But the lounge wasn't the quiet retreat she'd been hoping for. There must have been two dozen people gathered around Jill's husband, who saw Kaitlyn and began waving an instant-print photograph in the air. She made an excuse to the men and went over to see it.

"Two perfect little girls, born just after midnight," he said. "It was well worth missing the wedding."

She reached for the photograph. "That didn't take long," she said, with a half sigh of relief that it hadn't all happened in the church foyer. The babies were red faced and wrinkled, and each had a fuzz of dark hair. One of them appeared to be winking. "Obviously they're not camera shy," she murmured. "They're adorable!"

"Have a piece of bubble gum to celebrate. Unless you'd prefer a cigar? In fact, you should have two pieces. Oh, they're both girls, did I tell you?"

She couldn't smother her grin any longer. "You told me."

Marcus came up beside her with a frosty glass. "I thought you'd like a Tom Collins, darling," he said. "Long and cold. And a place to sit, of course." He indicated a chair and accepted a cigar from the proud new father. "You don't mind if I smoke, Kaitlyn?" He was already reaching into his pocket for a cigar clipper. He warmed the tip of the cigar over the candle flame in the center of the table, lighted it and leaned back with satisfaction as it began to glow red. "Now this isn't so bad, is it?"

Kaitlyn sipped her drink and then asked the waitress to bring her an iced tea instead. "What?"

"Being charming to my business associates, I mean. They like you a great deal. And they're very pleased at the idea of our marriage—the big management feels that married men are more stable." The two executives reappeared from the locker room, and Marcus summoned the waitress again to take their orders.

One of the men leaned back in his chair and said, "This is an amazing little town, Marcus. We never expected a boom like this when we bought the plant, you know."

Kaitlyn smiled. "And to think it can all be traced to just one company," she mused, "which only came to Springhill because the owner was trying to get his ex-wife back."

The senior of the executives looked at her rather pityingly. "Surely you're mistaken," he said. "That's not the way decisions are made in the world of business, Miss Ross."

"On the contrary," Kaitlyn muttered rebelliously. "You've probably met him this week." She certainly knew how the economy of this city had happened to turn around, because she had lived through it!—so she stopped listening to the executive.

That was probably why she heard the bits of conversation from the next table.

"You've seen the property—a weedy field with an old farmhouse falling down smack in the center of it," she heard one man say, and wondered idly why they were discussing the old Delaney place. It was an unsightly chunk of land just outside town—no, she remembered, it had become part of Springhill last year, when the city council had annexed the entire area.

"I certainly don't know why he wants it," another man at the table said. He sounded defensive. "He told me he was planning to drill for oil along the creek, but you know Penn."

"Maybe he just wants a matched set of run-down houses," the first man said with a laugh.

Kaitlyn frowned. Why on earth would Penn be trying to buy the Delaney place? It was certainly not in the hope of finding oil; that was precisely the kind of nonsense Penn would rattle off with a straight face if he didn't want to answer the question. But why was he buying anything in Springhill? It was crazy enough that he'd kept the lake cabin all these years....

"Kaitlyn," Marcus said impatiently. "What are you frowning about? You'd be delighted to have dinner with us, wouldn't you?"

She really ought to know better than to let her mind wander, she reflected. "Of course," she said quickly. "Though I'd like to freshen up first."

Marcus laughed fondly. "You'll have plenty of time for that, don't you think? The invitation is for Friday, Kaitlyn, when these gentlemen finish up with the plant inspections and all the work is done."

Her face flamed. "Of course," she said. "I—my thoughts must have just drifted off."

And if they didn't already think she was a classic dizzy female, Kaitlyn supposed she had just confirmed it. But at least it was a relief to know that Marcus wasn't expecting her to spend every evening with these two stuffed shirts—just Friday.

And Friday evening, she remembered too late, was to be the final rehearsal for Laura McCarthy's wedding on Saturday.

She didn't think it would help her image to beg off less than two minutes after accepting the invitation. So she kept silent and confessed the problem to Marcus when he took her home after another round of drinks.

"Surely the rehearsal won't last all night," he said tightly. "You'll just have to hurry it along and excuse yourself from the partying afterward. I'll push our dinner appointment back a little, and we'll make it work."

But it was obvious that he wasn't happy.

THE FLORIST looked frazzled, and he was half hoarse from screaming over the telephone at the supplier who had just informed him, less than four days before Laura McCarthy's wedding, that there would be no calla lilies for her bouquet. But no amount of yelling had changed the facts, so now he was sitting on the edge of a potting bench and shaking his head at Kaitlyn.

"I promised Laura calla lilies," he croaked. "And now there aren't any calla lilies to be had. Not by Saturday."

Kaitlyn pushed herself away from the cooler full of roses. "Then Laura will simply have to understand."

"I can't bring myself to tell her," the florist said frankly.

Kaitlyn sighed. "I'll break it to her. It's my job." She left the flower shop a few minutes later with the guarantee of amaryllis for Saturday and with a long-stemmed red rose, a gift from the grateful florist for not making him face the bride personally.

Thank heaven this didn't happen last week, she thought. Laura was levelheaded; she'd be disappointed, but she would understand. It if had been Sabrina, all hell would have broken loose.

She ran into Penn on the main square; he was coming down the courthouse steps as she was crossing the broad grassy lawn between the big old stone building and the street. There was really no way to pretend that she didn't see him, so she walked straight up to him and said, "Hello, Penn. How is the cabin coming along?"

His grin flashed. "Oh, it's fine. I'll buy you a milk-shake and tell you about it. Come on."

Great, Kaitlyn thought. She couldn't just say hello and keep walking; she had to put on social airs and graces and make conversation. And look where it had gotten her. Well, at least she could put off calling Laura.

He ushered her into the tiny restaurant on the corner, chose a high-backed booth, and ordered two double chocolate milkshakes.

Kaitlyn shook her head at the waitress. "Make mine club soda instead."

Penn nodded wisely. "I should have known. I suppose you'll be having to watch every calorie from now till after the wedding. I've got it. I'll get you a milkshake machine as my gift to the newlyweds. Afterward, it won't matter what your waistline looks like, so you can enjoy it."

"Thanks, Penn. But—"

"Unless you'd prefer something else. I had a rather nice African fertility charm once. I wonder where on earth I've left it?"

He might well have been speaking literally, Kaitlyn thought.

"Or I could always give you a full set of photos of the whole day. That's a gift worth thousands."

"Thousands? Don't push your luck. I still haven't seen the results from last weekend."

He grinned. "Why do you think I'm trying to get you to agree to the value before you have a chance to see the pictures? I know, how about a puppy?"

"I've got Schnoodle—at least Mother keeps reminding me that he's technically mine. Do you want a dog?"

"No."

"Of course you wouldn't—the way you travel around. You probably won't even be here by the time we get married. We decided on Valentine's Day."

"Poor Marcus," he said earnestly. "Keeping him waiting eight months, and not even moving in with him in the meantime."

Kaitlyn ignored that with an effort. "Maybe you won't even be invited," she pointed out. "Then you won't have to worry about a gift at all."

He looked thoughtful. "Perhaps I should try to be better friends with Marcus. Maybe he'll need an extra usher."

"And maybe not."

"True." Then his face lighted. "I guess I'd rather not be an usher, anyway—or take the pictures. I'll be your assistant coordinator."

"No, thanks."

"Kitten," he said earnestly, "you simply cannot be running around in your fancy gown to check on the proceedings. People would think it was strange. With me masterminding things, you could even have a glass or two of champagne at your own reception."

"I wouldn't dare."

He didn't seem to hear. "I think Marcus will like the idea. You'll be a lot more fun later if—"

She gritted her teeth, and then said firmly, "I thought you were going to tell me about the cabin."

"Oh, yes, I was, wasn't I? You should drive out and see it, actually. It's coming along very well—the furnace goes in next week."

She was reaching for her drink; her hand jerked, and the contents of her glass cascaded over the edge of the table and into her lap. She grabbed her napkin and began to scrub at her skirt.

"Now I see why you ordered club soda," Penn said.

"A furnace?" she managed to say. "Why do you need a furnace in a summer cabin?"

"You know, to supply heat. So I can live there in the winter, too, if I want."

"You're going to *live* there?"

"Kitten, I am already living there."

"No, I mean—year-round? Always?"

"Oh, probably not always," he said cheerfully.

"I see—you just like to keep your options open." She flung her soggy napkin aside. "That's the main thing that's wrong with you, Penn—do you know that? You don't want to choose anything because you might have to give up something else. And you don't finish anything, either, because before it's done, a more appealing project always comes along. You quit college after just a year; you haven't held a steady job since—"

He didn't answer, but at least he stopped drinking his milkshake and looked at her, eyebrows drawn together, as if he was truly listening.

After a moment she went on, more gently. "It was a rather attractive quality when you were younger, you know. You were always on the go, always doing something unexpected. It was exciting. But now it's just unfortunate. You had so much potential, Penn—" she broke off, fighting tears, and picked up her handbag. "Thanks for the drink."

"Is that why you've settled on Marcus?" He sounded merely interested, not annoyed or resentful.

She frowned till she saw the connection. "Because he's reliable? Of course not, though I will say it's nice to know I can always count on him."

"No," Penn said quietly. "That's not what I meant at all. I wouldn't marry you. Isn't that what you're really angry about, even after all this time? Isn't that why you're still cataloging my faults? Maybe if you'd take a good look at me, Kaitlyn—an honest look for a change—"

Kaitlyn bit her tongue, hard. "Damn you, Penn Caldwell," she said, her voice low and harsh. Then she turned on her heel and hurried out.

But his words seemed to echo in her head.

"I wouldn't marry you. Isn't that what you're really angry about, even after all this time?"

CHAPTER FIVE

THE SHEER EGO OF THE MAN, she stormed to herself as she dodged across the square toward her car. Ten blasted years had gone by, but Penn actually thought she was still concentrating on him after all that time—that she had even become engaged just to try to make him jealous! What a colossal fool he was. As if she hadn't had her share of attention from men in those ten years—and several of them had been quite willing to marry her, too. It certainly wasn't from lack of opportunity that she'd remained single—or because she was still mourning over her first, long-lost love, either. Penn was nothing more than a conceited blockhead to think that she had only accepted Marcus's proposal in order to prove to him that someone found her desirable after all.

The whole thing made her too furious even to scream.

The heels of her low pumps clicked out a staccato rhythm on the sun-washed sidewalk, almost matched by the angry pounding of blood in her ears, and the combination nearly drowned out the sound of her name being called from across the street. Eventually, however, she saw an arm waving frantically from the front door of the photographic studio, and she made her way cautiously through the traffic. The photographs of Sabrina's wedding must have been finished, she guessed. And if they were so bad that even the receptionist wanted to warn her...

"I thought you were never going to hear me," the young woman said. "I know you were anxious about those pictures so I dropped them off at Jill's house on my lunch hour."

"How were they?" Kaitlyn asked warily.

The receptionist shrugged. "Sorry, but I didn't even look at them. My job is to fetch and carry, not critique."

Kaitlyn retraced her steps to her car, and wondered whether it would be rude to simply drop in at Jill's house. She'd bought baby gifts for the twins just this morning, but she'd intended to wait a little while before going to visit. After all, Jill had only been home from the hospital for a couple of days, and had her hands full.

Jill's weathered-cedar house was nestled at the end of a quiet cul-de-sac, and a black Jaguar was parked in the driveway, so Kaitlyn stopped. If Stephanie was already there, at least she wouldn't be rousing Jill from a rest.

It was Stephanie who came to answer the door, in fact, with an infant cradled in her arms. "Sorry, Kaitlyn," she said. "But there aren't enough babies here to go round, and if you think I'm giving up this one, you're wrong. I'd like to take her home with me."

"I'll remember that," Jill called from the next room. "You may be picking her up about three o'clock some morning."

Kaitlyn followed the sound of Jill's voice into a big, casual living room with a cathedral ceiling. Jill was sitting in an oversize reclining chair holding a bottle for the other twin, the mirror image of her sister, fuzzy dark hair and all.

"How are you going to tell them apart?" Kaitlyn asked. She set a pair of pink wrapped boxes down beside Jill's chair and bent over the baby in fascination.

Jill sighed. "So far it's no problem; we never manage to put them both down at the same time. But I've already considered spray-painting their feet when they start to crawl—one red, one blue. The pictures are on the coffee table."

The babies were momentarily forgotten and Kaitlyn tossed her handbag down, seized the pile of fat envelopes and dropped onto the edge of the couch. Each of the hundred photographs was encased in a separate opaque envelope, and of the first half dozen that Kaitlyn pulled out, all were shots Jill had taken. Her hands were trembling by the time she found any of Penn's work.

"The woman has no taste," Stephanie was telling the twin she was holding. "She'd rather look at pictures than at you. Isn't she silly?" The baby yawned at her.

"They're not bad, altogether," Jill said. She shifted the twin she held over her shoulder and began to pat her back. "There's not a prizewinner in the bunch, but at least they're all in focus. I think if I'm careful—and a bit creative—in putting the proof album together, neither of us will be shot at dawn by the Harts."

"I'll start breathing again in a minute," Kaitlyn said. "After five days of being afraid to, I think I've forgotten how."

"Tell Penn if he wants a few pointers, I'll be happy to teach him. I might even offer him a part-time job if he wants it—we have to turn down weddings now because we can't be everywhere at once."

Kaitlyn set the stack of envelopes back on the coffee table with a sigh. "Better keep him as an emergency backup," she said. "He's a bit too unstable to rely on." There was more than a tinge of bitterness in her voice.

Stephanie stopped rocking the baby, and said quietly, "I should think most people would be a bit unstable, after the kind of shock Penn had. It's no wonder he went into a tailspin for a while."

Kaitlyn was almost ashamed of herself. Then she remembered that crazy accusation of his in the restaurant. Thinking she was still angry at him because he wouldn't marry her ten years ago, indeed! The man didn't have his thinking straightened out yet.

But she wasn't going to try to explain that bit of insight to Stephanie, so she said mildly, "If she's finished eating, Jill, may I hold her?" She picked the baby up cautiously. The infant's tiny, delicate dark eyebrows arched a little, and wide blue eyes studied Kaitlyn intently for a moment. Then they closed, and the rubbery little body sagged sleepily in her arms.

Jill stretched out in her chair with a sigh and reached for the boxes Kaitlyn had brought. "I think this is the first time in three days I haven't had at least one baby in my lap," she mused. "Or perhaps it's actually only been a matter of hours, and it simply feels like three days... What beautiful little dresses!" She stroked a delicate lace collar and added, "Where are you going to be moving, Kaitlyn?"

"I don't know."

Stephanie's brow furrowed. "The sale of the house closes in less than a week."

"Don't remind me," Kaitlyn said crisply. "I haven't forgotten that you'll be throwing me out onto the street next Monday morning with all my possessions in a shopping bag. At least it's summer; I won't freeze."

Stephanie winced. "I've been so busy I'd forgotten all about you," she admitted. "What about your mother?"

"She's found a place she likes, but it won't be available for a while—it needs repainting and new carpet. So she's going to stay with her sister in Omaha for a few weeks."

"Well, we'll find you something. Don't get desperate."

"Are you serious? I have a wedding to coordinate on Saturday and I have to move by Monday, and you say 'don't get desperate'?"

Stephanie shrugged. "You can always come and stay with us."

"You're not running a guest house. And don't forget my roomate—Schnoodle."

Jill stirred and opened her eyes. "We've got a cabin sitting empty up at Sapphire Lake. Why not go there for a month or so, till you can check things out?"

Kaitlyn considered it. She loved the lake, and in the summer, even a daily drive into town would be no more than a minor nuisance. Then she shook her head. "It's high season. You'll want to use it, and I'd be in your way."

Jill looked from the sleeping infant in Kaitlyn's arms to the one Stephanie held, and said frankly, "I'm not planning to throw any wild parties up there this summer. In fact, if I have my choice between packing up these little darlings and hauling them and all their equipment up to the lake, or staying home with my air conditioner and dishwasher—"

Kaitlyn nodded. "I see your point. All right, Jill, I'll take you up on it—and thanks; you're a lifesaver. In a week or two things will settle down, and then I can look around."

Jill yawned. "I'll get you the key if I can work up the energy to crawl out of this chair."

Stephanie smiled. "I suppose this lazy attitude means you aren't interested in an impromptu skating party tonight, Jill?"

"Roller skates, you mean?" Kaitlyn asked. "You're taking a bunch of kids, right?"

"Of course, but the kids are only an excuse. You'll come, won't you?"

"I haven't been on skates in years, Steph."

"Neither have the rest of us. Come on, it'll be fun." Stephanie glanced down at the twin in her arms. "Oops, this one went out like a light, too. And Jill has drifted off to dreamland as well, I see. . . . Shall we tuck everyone in for a nap?"

She led the way upstairs to the twins' nursery, where two identical white bassinets stood side by side. "Now, I need to get this straight," Stephanie mused. "I was holding Jessica—wasn't I?"

"They're adorable," Kaitlyn murmured. "But Jill looks exhausted."

"Yes, for the moment. But there's nothing like a tiny trusting infant nestled against your breast to make you regret that they grow up. You'll see what I mean, someday. If you need help getting moved up to the cabin, Kaitlyn—"

"It will have to be Sunday, I suppose," Kaitlyn said. "But I won't be taking much except my clothes, so I think I can handle it myself. Talking about cabins reminds me, though. Is Penn really trying to buy the old Delaney place?"

Stephanie's face remained perfectly pleasant and calm, but she raised her eyebrows in puzzlement. "The Delaney place?"

"Stephanie, I've learned to recognize that professionally blank look of yours. It means he is, otherwise you'd have looked surprised. Why does he want it, anyway?"

Stephanie relented with a shrug. "He hasn't told me; I'm only the go-between. But I expect he plans to build a house."

"Well, at least that makes more sense than the last tale I heard—" Kaitlyn gulped as Stephanie's words sank in. She didn't say a word until they were back downstairs, and then all she could manage was, "Why here?"

"Why *not* here? Springhill certainly needs houses; there are people standing in line to buy them. It's a great opportunity for someone like Penn."

"Oh. You mean he's going to build a house just to sell it?" For a minute there, Kaitlyn admitted, she'd been really worried. Having Penn around Springhill on a more-or-less permanent basis wouldn't be very comfortable at all.

Stephanie nodded. "That seems to be the idea."

There was an odd tremor of relief in the pit of Kaitlyn's stomach. "I'm not surprised. Penn wouldn't be likely to settle down here. I wonder if he'll even manage to stay interested long enough for the contractors to finish it."

"Kaitlyn, he's been building houses for several years. And it's not a question of contractors. He does it himself—the whole process."

Kaitlyn blinked in surprise. "You mean the sawing and the nailing and everything?"

"He can't manage all the heavy work alone, but—"

"And just where has he been doing this?"

"All over the country. He builds a house, sells it and moves on."

"I see. I'm glad you didn't expect me to believe that all this time he's actually been a solid citizen and a member of the Chamber of Commerce somewhere. What about all the other strange occupations I've heard about?"

Stephanie said impatiently, "Oh, he's done every one of those things, and probably a whole lot more. Not many people know everything Penn's done."

"And now he's building houses. Well, isn't that just like Penn?" Kaitlyn asked indignantly. "A carpenter who builds a house and then takes off for parts unknown. Most people would stay in one place and establish a reputation—unless, of course, the houses he builds fall down, or turn out to be so strange that no one wants to live in them."

"Penn is not *most people*, Kaitlyn." Stephanie looked annoyed. "Is it really such an odd thing to do? With the size of the estate his parents left, Penn doesn't have to earn a living, you know. What does it matter if he takes an unusual approach to work? Or if he doesn't want to stay in one place, either?" She released a long, exasperated breath. "Think about it, honey—you may conclude it's not so crazy, after all. At least it's not to Penn."

"Nothing," Kaitlyn said, "sounds too crazy for Penn!"

SHE FINISHED HER ERRANDS, picking up the cocktail napkins for Laura McCarthy's reception, breaking the news to her about the calla lilies, checking that the tuxedos would be available when promised at the rental place, sampling the icing that the bakery planned to use on the cake. Finally she was ready to go home and face an evening of packing.

She went in through the garden gate and stood thoughtfully testing it out. It was now properly square on its hinges with not a squeak to be heard. That had been quite a tool kit Penn had brought along the day he'd come to fix it. And the tools hadn't been new—they were certainly not the ones she'd seen him buying at the hardware store. She hadn't realized till now that she had even noticed.

Perhaps Penn wasn't quite such a complacent drifter. She might have been wrong—partially, at least. And he had managed to save her neck with those wedding pictures. Did she owe him an apology?

"About the same time he makes me one," she muttered, and went inside.

Audrey Ross was in the kitchen, putting pots and pans into boxes. "I've got no idea what to do with all this stuff," she said. "I've sorted out a few things for you, Kaitlyn, for your new kitchen." She waved a hand toward the table, which was piled high.

"I've already got everything I need, Mother—boxed up in the attic, where we put it all when I moved back home. Remember?"

Momentarily, Audrey looked puzzled, but then she said, "Oh, yes, of course. You're right. Then what shall I do with all of this? There won't be room for it in my apartment."

"Put it in Stephanie's garage and leave it. Maybe she'll have a tag sale eventually."

Audrey laughed. "Wait till you see the things I found today, darling. The teddy bear you made when you were in third grade and the dress you wore to the senior prom. It still has the rip in it where Penn stepped on the hem."

Penn, again. Well, she wasn't going to get drawn into reminiscences with her mother tonight, that was certain. "I'm going to the attic to look for those boxes," she said, and told her mother about Jill's offer of the cabin.

"Oh, that's good. I was beginning to worry about you. Try the southwest corner; I think I saw boxes there with your name on them."

The attic was hot, and it had the characteristically musty smell that always made Kaitlyn want to sneeze. She climbed the folding stairs and turned on the dim lights and looked around in amazement. Her mother had been working miracles up here; the shelves and nooks full of clutter had been reduced to neatly labeled boxes, piled and sorted and ready to be moved.

The stack of boxes in the southwest corner did indeed bear Kaitlyn's name, and little else in the way of information; now that she stopped to think about it, she remembered packing up her apartment in such a hurry that she hadn't bothered to properly label each carton.

She growled a little in disgust at her own carelessness. Jill's cabin up at Sapphire Lake was one of the smaller ones. Unlike Stephanie's elaborate summer home, which was always ready for a party of any size, Jill's was equipped more for occasional picnics than for full-time living. If Kaitlyn was going to be there for at least a month she'd need some of her own things. The problem was going to be knowing in precisely which boxes she would find them.

Well, she'd just have to take them all, she supposed. If she didn't, the one she most needed was certainly to end up at the bottom of a pile of her mother's things in a warehouse somewhere.

Perhaps I acted a little too quickly in turning down Stephanie's offer of help, she thought. *All these boxes...*

Audrey's head appeared at the top of the stairs. "You're not going to work tonight, surely?"

"Why wouldn't I? I've hardly given you any help at all."

"Oh, don't worry about that; I've got everything arranged. Penn said you were going skating."

"Oh, he did?" Had that been before or after their quarrel? she wondered. Not that it really mattered; it was time she and Penn got a few things straightened out.

Kaitlyn glanced at her wristwatch and went back downstairs to change into jeans and freshen her makeup.

Penn was just going to have to stop doing things like this! Telling her mother that she was going skating, before Kaitlyn had even known it herself—making it appear like some sort of date they'd made! Who else had he told?

It annoyed her that in order to talk to him she would in a sense be confirming what he'd told Audrey—she'd have to go to the rink, at least. But there was no sense in waiting; it might be days before she had another free evening, and then she might not know where to find Penn.

The roller-skating rink had once been at the very edge of Springhill, before the town had grown up around it. Now it lay between the industrial park and a whole new shopping complex. It was not particularly busy on a summer Wednesday, and she had no trouble spotting the party. Penn was on the far side of the oval rink with Stephanie's little girl, trying to convince her to come out onto the floor with him.

Kaitlyn laced up her skates and said hello to the rink's owner as she paid her admission fee. "Just like old times, isn't it?" he said with a smile. "All you guys used to hang around here on Saturday nights and give me headaches."

She took a few short, tentative steps on the glass-smooth floor. It took a moment to regain her balance, but skating was like riding a bicycle, really, she told herself. The knowledge might be tucked away unused, but it could never be forgotten. It would, however, take time and practice if she was to get back the confidence she had once had, and she found herself staying very close to the rail as she made her way around the rink for the first time.

Penn came up behind her with a swoop and slowed to keep pace. He looked down at her appraisingly, with his head tipped a little to one side, hands clasped behind his back. "I didn't think you'd come, after that fight."

She put her chin up. "I never miss a skating party if I can help it. It's got nothing to do with you."

"Oh? I thought perhaps you'd thought of a few more things you wanted to tell me."

"Things I'd forgotten to bring up this afternoon?" She shook her head. "I shouldn't have said what I did, Penn. I'm sorry."

The tight line of his jaw relaxed, and in the same instant the music changed and softened. The owner hadn't been kidding about remembering those long-ago Saturday nights, Kaitlyn thought. That had been one of their favorite songs, ten years ago.

And don't start getting sentimental, she told herself.

"A bit ungracious," he mused, "but it will do."

"Now wait just a minute while I make myself clear," she warned. "I didn't say I'd changed my mind—just that it's none of my business what you do with your life."

Penn's eyebrows rose a fraction.

"And of course it's equally true that what I do with my life is none of your affair."

"Oh, absolutely," he murmured.

"I'll appreciate it if you remember that in the future. And of course I accept your apology for interfering—"

"If that makes you happy," he said earnestly, "I certainly don't object. Now that we have all that straightened out, come skate with me. I mean really skate, not this clinging-to-the-rail stuff."

She shook her head. "I have things to do tonight."

He glanced around the rink. "Leave now, and everyone in the place will think we've just quarreled. And they'll start wondering why."

She hadn't considered that. But he was probably right, she thought.

"If you stay, we'll just be two old friends skating. Surely not even Marcus could object to that—could he?"

"I suppose you told him I'd be here, so he would drop by and be scandalized."

Penn looked rather shocked. "And interfere with your life? Of course not. Unless—are we going to be doing something scandalous, Kitten?"

She glared at him.

"No? Then why would I want Marcus?" He shrugged. "I'd bet any amount of cash he's no fun at all on skates."

"I may not be, either," she warned. "I'm out of practice."

"Well, you won't get any better as long as you hang on to the rail. Come on, Kitten. I won't let you fall."

He gave her a brilliant smile as she released her death grip and slowly reached out to him. Penn's hands were warm as they closed gently over hers, and for the first few minutes they simply swept along, catching the rhythm of the music and translating it into their stride. It was fun— she had forgotten how much fun—to swoop and glide and almost float around the rink.

Penn spun her around till she was skating backward, at arm's length from him, with her elbows locked. She couldn't help stealing a fearful glance over her shoulder, though she knew the movement was almost guaranteed to break the rhythm of her stride and send her spinning.

His hold tightened reassuringly, and slowly he began to draw her closer, until their clasped hands were pressed virtually against his chest.

The lyrics of the song, the vibration that tingled up from her toes through her entire body, the warmth of his hands holding hers, all brought back such strong memories that they conspired to leave Kaitlyn practically breathless. The music was loud, and the drone of a hundred skates made it too difficult to talk, and so they only swept along together, hands clasped, alone in a bubble of silence within the noisy rink.

Then the music slowed slightly, and segued into a softer, gentler rhythm. "Do you still remember how to waltz on skates?" Penn asked.

Remember? she thought. How could I ever forget waltzing with you? Here—and also at the prom that night, for one brief number before we were caught and almost thrown out of the ballroom....

This is dangerous, Kaitlyn told herself. I must stop this now. I must get back to safer ground—I must break this spell.

"*Me* remember?" she protested lightly. "You're the one who ruined an expensive dress because you lost track of your feet and stepped on the hem."

"Slander. Sheer slander. I did not lose track of my feet; I knew exactly where my feet were. It was the dress that got in the wrong place. Good thing you're not wearing one tonight." He shifted his grip slightly and drew her closer still. "Ready?"

One waltz, she thought, *and then I'm going home.*

She'd forgotten how much concentration it took to maintain her balance in the sweeping turns, and to keep her steps in perfect rhythm with his. In an ordinary ballroom, a minor error might mean a stepped-on toe, but here on the rink the same small glitch could send both partners tumbling into the wall. Being kicked by a roller skate was no small injury, and it had happened to each of them more than once, when they'd first started practicing.

Kaitlyn noticed vaguely that the crowd around them seemed to be thinning out, but it wasn't until the music had slowed and stopped, and they glided to a halt at the rail, that she realized that they had finished the waltz entirely alone. There was a smattering of applause, and she flashed a grin at Penn and went automatically into her favorite trick—a low bow and spin. But something went radically wrong, and she ended up sprawled on the highly polished floor, with the breath knocked out of her.

Penn looked down at her dispassionately. "I was going to suggest that if we worked hard enough at it we could do a polka," he said. "But if you're just going to lie around on the floor like this, Kitten—"

"I might as well," she gasped. "My timing is shot."

He smiled and hauled her to her feet, and as the music picked up again, he drew her back into his arms and pushed away from the wall, and she forgot altogether that she had been intending to leave.

When the music stopped for the final time, and the lights came up to normal, Kaitlyn was startled to see how few skaters remained.

"All the kids had to go home to meet curfew," Penn said. "It's one of the advantages of being a grown-up."

Kaitlyn glanced at the clock and shook her head in surprise. "I had no idea it was so late. Where's Stephanie and the rest of the crowd?"

Penn shrugged. "That's one of the *disadvantages* of being a grown-up—they had to take all the kids home." He gave her a crooked grin.

They made one last slow circle of the rink, and the benches at the entrance were empty by the time they sat down to remove their skates. Even the rink's owner had gone to the far end of the building to begin turning off the lights, so they were alone.

Kaitlyn extracted her foot from her right boot and winced at the burning tenderness in her heel. "I'm going to have blisters," she groaned.

"Let me see." Penn lifted her foot into his lap. "You're right—you must have had a wrinkle in your sock."

"Thank you for the expert diagnosis, Dr. Caldwell," she said sweetly, and tried to pull away.

He held on to her foot with both hands and began to massage the sole. His touch was firm and strong as he worked from the base of her toes across the ball of her foot. When he reached the more sensitive instep, she wriggled and had to brace herself with her hands clasped on the edge of the bench to keep from losing her balance. "That tickles, Penn," she protested.

But he did not let go, just sat there cradling her foot in the palm of his hand, looking at her. The gray of his eyes had gone dark and smoky.

Kaitlyn felt her heart thud alarmingly as he started to lean toward her. A kiss for old times' sake—she could hear him saying it, even though he hadn't made a sound.

"No," she whispered.

"You're still the most kissable girl in Springhill," he replied softly.

You taught me that, she thought. *You taught me long and patiently...*

"Don't try to bring back those easy days of summer, Penn," she said. "They're gone. We're different people now. So—just let those memories rest in peace."

His grip loosened—more in surprise, she thought, than agreement. Kaitlyn shoved her feet into her street shoes and pushed her skates into her tote bag and jumped up.

Peace, she thought, *for the moment.* But it seemed likely that it would be an uneasy peace.

CHAPTER SIX

THE HOTEL COFFEE SHOP was Kaitlyn's favorite place to have breakfast; she often brought her clients here for a final conference a day or two before their wedding. The tables were big enough to spread paperwork out, the omelettes were the best in a hundred miles and the coffee came in large, thick mugs supplemented by a thermal pot, so it was never necessary to wait for a refill. The coffee shop wasn't particularly classy, but that was all to the good, too. With the hours counting down to the wedding, with all the elegant arrangements made and nothing left to do for the next forty-eight hours but worry, the bride was often nervous enough to upset her orange juice or pour syrup all over herself. At least at the coffee shop it did no real damage.

Kaitlyn glanced through the neatly written pages that held every important detail about Laura McCarthy's wedding, and transferred a couple of notes to her list of things to do today. She was so absorbed that for a moment she didn't hear the man who stopped beside her table, and finally he repeated, "Kaitlyn, darling, do you mind if I join you?" His hand hovered above the chair next to hers, but it was a formality, just one more example of Marcus's beautiful manners.

Kaitlyn looked up from the folder. "Oh—no, I wouldn't mind at all, except that I'm waiting for a couple of clients."

NO RISK, NO OBLIGATION TO BUY ... NOW OR EVER!

CASINO JUBILEE
"Scratch'n Match" Game

Here's how to play:

1. Peel off label from front cover. Place it in space provided at right. With a coin, carefully scratch off the silver box. This makes you eligible to receive two or more free books, and possibly other gifts, depending upon what is revealed beneath the scratch-off area.

2. You'll receive brand-new Harlequin Romance® novels. When you return this card, we'll rush you the books and gifts you qualify for, ABSOLUTELY FREE!

3. If we don't hear from you, every month we'll send you 6 additional novels to read and enjoy months before they are available in bookstores. You can return them and owe nothing, but if you decide to keep them, you'll pay only $2.49* per book, a saving of 40¢ each off the cover price. There is **no** extra charge for postage and handling. There are **no** hidden extras.

4. When you join the Harlequin Reader Service®, you'll get our subscribers-only newsletter, as well as additional free gifts from time to time, just for being a subscriber!

5. You must be completely satisfied. You may cancel at any time simply by sending us a note or a shipping statement marked "cancel" or by returning any shipment to us at our cost.

YOURS FREE!

This lovely heart-shaped box is richly detailed with cut-glass decorations, perfect for holding a precious memento or keepsake—and it's yours absolutely free when you accept our no-risk offer.

CASINO JUBILEE
"Scratch'n Match" Game

CHECK CLAIM CHART BELOW
FOR YOUR FREE GIFTS!

YES! I have placed my label from the front cover in the space provided above and scratched off the silver box. Please send me all the gifts for which I qualify. I understand I am under no obligation to purchase any books, as explained on the opposite page.

(U-H-R-08/92) 116 CIH AFN7

Name _____

Address _____ Apt. _____

City _____ State _____ Zip _____

CASINO JUBILEE CLAIM CHART	
🍒🍒🍒	WORTH 4 FREE BOOKS, FREE HEART-SHAPED CURIO BOX PLUS MYSTERY BONUS GIFT
🍒🍒🔔	WORTH 3 FREE BOOKS PLUS MYSTERY GIFT
🔔🔔🍒	WORTH 2 FREE BOOKS CLAIM Nº **1528**

◀ DETACH AND MAIL CARD TODAY! ▶

HARLEQUIN "NO RISK" GUARANTEE

Marcus's lips tightened slightly. "I see. New ones?"

"No, they're almost-finished ones. It's a last-minute conference so I can check details once more and give them a final pep talk."

"Of course." His tone was faintly ironic. "Then I'll just sit down a moment until they arrive."

Kaitlyn suppressed a sigh and put the folder out of sight. It didn't matter, she told herself. She knew everything that was in there, anyway. She ought to; she'd certainly been over it often enough. There had to be a way to cut down the sheer amount of time she spent fussing over each ceremony, she thought. But if she stopped being such a perfectionist, then upsets like the mess at Sabrina Hart's wedding would happen much more often.

That idea was enough to make her shiver and be even more determined not to overlook anything.

"What about after breakfast?" Marcus said. "I've got an easy morning, so I could be flexible."

She looked at him in astonishment. "I thought your friendly executives were still hanging around."

"They are. But they've hinted I really ought to get out of the office a little more—do some volunteer work, be seen around the community, make a few more contacts. Perhaps we could play nine holes of golf or something."

Kaitlyn shook her head. "I'm sorry, but I've got a preliminary conference with the Wagners today. They're celebrating their fiftieth wedding anniversary in a few months."

Marcus's voice had a rough edge. "You suggested yourself that I take a morning off now and then so we could see each other, Kaitlyn," he reminded her.

"But I certainly didn't say I was always free, any morning at random! If you had asked ahead of time, I probably could have rearranged my calendar. I'm very busy this week—''

"Not too busy to spend last evening on skates."

His voice was cool, and every muscle in Kaitlyn's body tensed. She wanted to ask him how he knew—was Penn interfering again?—but she knew better; the question alone would make her look guilty.

"Honestly, Kaitlyn, of all the middle-class pastimes, roller skating has got to be at the head of the list."

He made it sound like something slightly off-color, Kaitlyn thought—in the same category as belly dancing.

"No," she said pointedly, "I'd say that bowling is the primary middle-class hobby. And I happen to like that, too. I'm sorry if it upsets you, but I guess I'm just middle class, Marcus. I was born that way. My father worked on a manufacturing line, and—"

"Darling, I'm sorry. Of course I didn't mean that there was anything wrong with you, or with your background. You'll learn to enjoy other things, as well, I'm sure, when you have a chance to experience them."

She ground her teeth together, but she didn't answer.

"And of course you need to relax." He put his hand over her fingers, which lay rigid on the edge of the table. "I'm glad you had a good time last night, truly I am. It was unforgivable of me to lose my temper like that." He smiled down at her. "I'm just a bit irritable this morning, I suppose. We were trying to get some serious matters taken care of at the club last night, and there was a very noisy party in the next room. It left me with a pounding headache that still hasn't gone away entirely."

She didn't quite trust herself to answer, but fortunately, she didn't have to; Laura and her fiancé arrived just then. Marcus rose and shook hands with the young man. "I was just on my way," he explained punctiliously. "Jack Bailey—now where…? Oh, you were the one having the party at the country club last night." His glance at Kaitlyn was expressive.

"It was Jack's bachelor party," Laura said curtly, and Marcus nodded as if that explained a lot.

Kaitlyn eyed the young man over the edge of her menu, which she could practically recite by heart. Jack Bailey looked a little worse for wear this morning, as if he'd been up far too late last night and had too much to drink, as well. A bachelor party in the middle of the week? That was strange. But she supposed it made sense, since most of Jack's family and friends were from out of town, for them to come a few days early instead of making the trip twice.

He ordered only coffee, which confirmed her suspicions, and sat silent through most of the discussion. Laura, too, was quieter than usual, Kaitlyn thought, and only picked at her food. Well, every bride reacted differently; it was one of the things Kaitlyn liked best about her business.

Kaitlyn finished her omelette and checked her list again. "Have you received any last-minute responses?" she asked.

Laura pulled a handful of cards from her handbag.

Kaitlyn flipped through them. "I'll do a count and get a final number to the caterer today," she said almost to herself. "You'll need to pick up your tuxedo, Jack, and remind your ushers to pick up theirs. Make sure they try everything on, too. Rental places make mistakes sometimes, and it's much easier to get trousers rehemmed today than it will be on Saturday."

"Oh," he said. "Sure."

Kaitlyn would have liked to pour coffee on him, just to see if he was paying attention to any external stimuli at all.

Instead, she turned to Laura. "You've broken in your shoes and practiced doing your makeup and hair style?"

Laura nodded.

"Then the only thing left for you to do is relax and enjoy yourself and get your attendants to the rehearsal on time," Kaitlyn told her with a smile. "I won't keep you any longer." She put her pen down and closed the folder.

Jack Bailey jumped up, brushed a quick kiss on his bride's cheek, and hurried out, muttering something about getting to work. *So much for the tuxedos,* Kaitlyn thought. *I'll probably end up getting them myself, and passing them out at the rehearsal tomorrow. We'll just have to hope they fit....*

"I'll remind the ushers," Laura said quietly.

Kaitlyn debated with herself while she paid the bill, and finally said, "Is everything all right between you two?"

Laura didn't look quite squarely at her. "Sure. Jack's got a lot on his mind." But it was almost halfhearted, as if it was herself she was really trying to convince.

Kaitlyn nodded. "You've had a fight." It wasn't a question.

Laura's chin wobbled a little. She bit her lip and whispered, "Last night."

Over the bachelor party, no doubt. A party loud enough to penetrate the entire country club must have included more than enough drinking and general nonsense to upset a bride who was already sensitive and on edge. It wasn't the first time such a thing had happened; it was bad judgment on Jack Bailey's part, perhaps, but no more than that.

"I see," Kaitlyn said gently. "It's not unusual, you know. Practically every couple has a zinger of a fight not long before the wedding." As a matter of fact, she thought, remembering the way she and Marcus had snapped at each other this morning, sometimes it doesn't even have to be close to the wedding day.

"Do they?" Laura asked.

"It doesn't mean you aren't suited, you know. Or that you shouldn't be married."

"That's what my mother says. That I should just ignore it, I mean."

"Well, she's right." Kaitlyn patted Laura's shoulder. "It's only tension, you know. It builds up till something has to give, that's all. Some people have that fight at the church. Others manage to hold it off till after the wedding, and then have a tremendous blowup on their honeymoon. That would be a whole lot worse."

"I suppose so."

"Perhaps you and Jack are lucky to get it over with now." There was a reassuring smile in Kaitlyn's voice. "Have a good time at your bridesmaids' lunch."

Laura nodded, and Kaitlyn stood on the sidewalk in front of the hotel for a long time, watching till she was out of sight. She suddenly felt almost exhausted.

The things I do for my brides, she thought. She could hang out a shingle as a premarriage counselor, on top of everything else. Perhaps Marcus was right, after all, about how difficult it would be to balance everything. After this wedding was over, she was going to have to do some serious thinking about where she wanted to go from here.

THE ROSS HOME was beginning to look like a warehouse, with boxes piled to the ceiling on every corner and no flat surface bare of clutter. Kaitlyn managed to clear the kitchen table of the pots, pans, bowls and baking sheets that filled it by simply dumping them into several big cartons and writing Salvation Army in bold black letters on the sides. Then she piled the boxes against a wall, washed

her hands and spread out the computerized address list for
Kathy Warren's wedding. It wasn't until September, but it
would probably take a full week to address all of the invitations, Kaitlyn thought as she opened the boxes of stationery and filled her calligraphy pen with ink. Still, it
wasn't as big an affair as Sabrina Hart's had been...thank
heaven.

She lined the boxes up and began. The invitation itself.
The cover sheet of tissue. The response card, with its own
small stamped envelope. The second invitation, where
needed, to the dinner reception. The inner envelope, with
only the names neatly lettered. The outer envelope, carefully addressed and sealed. And, at long last, the name
checked off the list.

She set the thick packet aside and said, "One down. A
mere 499 to go."

Behind her, Penn said, "From the sound of that, this
must be the boring part."

Kaitlyn jumped and dropped her pen. Ink splattered,
but fortunately it missed the expensive engraving.

He wasn't wearing a shirt at all today, and his bronzed
skin looked damp—almost shiny. There were streaks of
dust and what looked like oil here and there on his arms
and chest, and his jeans were filthy. But despite the surface dirt, he smelled of soap and the warmth of summer
days.

You've got summer on the brain, Kaitlyn told herself.

"Are those the invitations to your wedding?" He leaned
over her shoulder to look more closely at her work.

"Dammit, Penn, don't you dare touch these things,"
she ordered, and threw her arms across the piles of invitations covering the table. "Of course they're not for my
wedding—it's far too early."

"I thought you might have moved it up." He read the finely engraved script. "And I just wanted to be sure you didn't forget about sending one to me."

"I couldn't possibly forget you," Kaitlyn grumbled.

He smiled, and sketched a bow. "Thank you for the compliment. I'm relieved to know that I won't have to follow the mailman around, asking if he might have mislaid my invitation."

He'd do it, too, she thought. If, of course, he was still in Springhill—but there was no point in worrying about it now. "What have you been up to, anyway? You look as if you've been crawling through a coal mine."

"That's close," he congratulated her. "I'm cleaning out the basement. Your mother didn't think the movers should pack up every half-used can of paint and every scrap of wood in your father's workshop, but she wasn't sure what to keep."

"Oh—is that why the pickup truck full of junk is blocking the driveway so I couldn't get in?" She should have known he'd be driving something of the sort, she thought. She supposed he needed it when he was working on a house. And it was quite appropriate, actually, for a man who cared so little about material possessions. Still, for Penn Caldwell to be getting around in a faded, half-rusted-out truck—

"Would you rather I blocked the drive so you couldn't get *out?*" He took a newspaper-wrapped tumbler from a box, tossed the paper into another box and filled the glass with ice and water. He perched on the edge of the counter and studied her, one foot swinging.

She watched the play of muscles in his arm and chest as he drank, and wondered what he'd look like when he was lifting something heavy. Enough, she told herself, and turned back to her invitations.

"Audrey thought perhaps I could use some of the tools and things," Penn went on.

Kaitlyn didn't look up. "So now you're running a salvage operation? I'm not surprised."

"Not exactly. Didn't you know that your mother has a soft touch for a bum? She's going to give me a plate of leftovers for this."

"Funny. Very funny."

He got up to refill his glass and inspected the scanty contents of the refrigerator. "I see the joke's on me," he said mournfully. "Are you and Audrey living on cold cuts these days? But since you haven't paid me for those photographs yet, I don't have much choice. If I'm going to eat at all—"

"I offered you standard pay."

He leaned around the refrigerator door and looked her over speculatively. "Kitten, don't be silly. If I hadn't come to the rescue, Mrs. Hart would have made sausage hors d'oeuvres out of you. That's got to be worth more than ordinary wages."

"So send me a bill. We can negotiate."

Penn looked thoughtful. "All right. I'll start at a million bucks."

Kaitlyn didn't even glance up. "I think there's a twenty in my wallet. Take it or leave it."

"Well, we certainly have lots of room for compromise." Penn washed his hands, then took the package of cold cuts from the refrigerator and unearthed a loaf of bread from under the packing supplies stacked on top of the dishwasher. "Seriously, though, do you mind if Audrey gives me some of your dad's tools?"

"Why would I mind? I'm not into drills and saws and whatever else he had down there."

Penn shrugged. "I thought it was possible Marcus might be coveting them." Possible, the tone seemed to say, but hardly likely, considering that it's Marcus, after all.

Kaitlyn refused to take offense. If Penn wanted to believe that no man could be truly masculine without being comfortable in a woodworking shop, that was his problem—certainly not hers. "I don't think Marcus has ever been in that basement, so I doubt he's given the contents any thought at all. You're welcome to take the works." She smiled. "Just knock the value off what I owe you for the pictures, all right?"

Penn snapped his fingers. "I've got it. Wait till you hear this. Have I got a deal for you—"

"Hold it a minute." Kaitlyn spelled a troublesome name out letter by letter as she addressed an envelope, and then set it aside and leaned back in her chair. "All right. Let me have it."

"You and Marcus will need somewhere to live after you're married, right? And I've got a nice little piece of property."

So he'd gotten the Delaney place, after all, she thought. No wonder Stephanie had been too busy this week to remember that Kaitlyn needed an apartment. "And you're suggesting that you build a house for Marcus and me? No, thanks."

"I'll just add the cost of the pictures on top of the building," he added helpfully. "Marcus will never notice it. Not the full million, of course; I'll give you a break on that."

"I'm touched," she said dryly. Kaitlyn could almost hear what Marcus would have to say about the idea of Penn building a house for them. "But no thanks. We won't be interested in building for a couple of years at least."

"What's the matter? Has Marcus overreached himself and ruined his credit rating?"

"Of course not! But in a year or two we'll know more about our lifestyle, and the way we want to live."

"I get it. Whether you want to have kids and all. Do you?"

"You don't think I'd discuss the question with you, surely?"

"Well, it was worth a try, Kitten—not the kids, the house. It might be fun, for a change, to know who I was building for."

"You mean you generally don't?"

Penn shook his head. "No. I just build a house and when it's done, it goes up for sale."

"And that *works?* Good heavens, Penn—"

"But it would have been interesting to keep you in mind, and puzzle out the way you'd like things. You ought to think about my offer, Kitten. It's the only way you'll get a say in the house Marcus builds."

She put her pen down and stared at him incredulously. "What on earth do you mean?"

"Don't tell me you haven't noticed. He complains whenever I call you Kitten, but he actually treats you like one—a fluffy little female who only knows how to be helpless." He finished off his sandwich.

"How perfectly ridiculous."

"You think you're making all the plans for your wedding, don't you?"

"I'm consulting Marcus, of course, but—"

"And I'll bet he allows you to arrange things until it interferes with his plans, and then he'll put his foot down. Take your honeymoon—"

"And just what would you know about my honeymoon, Penn?"

"You still don't know where you're going? I do. Marcus has already made up his mind. I asked him last night—not straight out, of course—and he told me."

Kaitlyn didn't like the sound of that. Just how had he extracted that sort of information from Marcus? "I thought you weren't going to interfere in my life anymore."

"I didn't. The bachelor party going on in the next room seemed to inspire our Marcus to tell us all how it should be done. Perhaps you should take him on as a partner, Kitten. I can see it now—Socially Correct Weddings by the Wainwrights. Your mother doesn't like him, by the way."

"Oh? Have you taken up reading minds?"

"No. She told me."

"It's nice that you two are so close. But I must warn you that Mother has been a little confused lately. Just yesterday she told me that you're keeping the cabin so you can hold clan reunions there someday. *What* clan, I asked her—"

It was out before she stopped to think, and only when she saw the smoky gray of his eyes shift and darken almost to black did she recognize the cruelty of those thoughtless words, reminding him of how alone he was. "I'm sorry, Penn," she whispered. "Oh, dear heaven, I'm sorry—"

"Why be sorry for the truth? Facts is facts," he said ungrammatically. "Would you like me to tell you where you're going on your honeymoon?"

"Of course I would." She kept her voice level, careless—and she didn't glance up from the invitation she was assembling.

Penn came across the kitchen to her, and his palm cupped warmly against her chin and made her look at him. His gaze searched her face.

She didn't try to look away. "But I'm not going to kiss you to get this information, Penn," she said sweetly. "I'll just ask Marcus."

"And you really think he'd tell you?" he scoffed. He flicked the tip of her nose with his index finger. "Bermuda."

"In February? It's still too cold—" Her voice was slightly squeaky for an instant, and then the shock passed. "He must have been leading you on."

"Nope. Marcus is not capable of that sort of joke. Aren't you going to thank me? At least you'll know what sort of clothes to pack." He started to build himself another sandwich. "But then perhaps Marcus doesn't intend to let you out of the honeymoon suite, so it won't matter whether you have any clothes at all."

"Please, Penn. You're so distressingly crude."

"Well, I certainly wouldn't."

He looked at her levelly, over the stack of rye bread and turkey and cheese, and Kaitlyn felt her insides go liquid. Once, she had dreamed of sharing a honeymoon suite with Penn. And she hadn't concerned herself with what scenery might be visible outside it, either.

"If I ever found anyone I was nuts enough to marry, that is," he added casually.

Kaitlyn waited till her heartbeat had slowed to normal. "Well, that isn't likely, is it?" she said repressively. "Because it isn't only you who'd have to be nuts, Penn."

SHE HAD NEVER ORGANIZED a wedding rehearsal yet where everyone was on time, and Laura McCarthy's was no exception. Normally it was no real problem. If the members of the wedding party were late and took longer than necessary in learning their parts, they were really only inconveniencing themselves, for it was their own after-rehearsal dinner that was being delayed.

But tonight was a bit different. Kaitlyn had a dinner date to keep, and she wanted, at all costs, to be on time. She wasn't ready to have another discussion with Marcus on the future of her business—not until she'd had a chance to think it out for herself, at least.

So when the best man showed up at St. Matthew's a full twenty minutes late, she greeted him briskly and turned directly back to the ushers to finish her instructions. "Each adult is to get a candle as he or she is seated, along with the wedding program. But use your common sense," she pleaded. "If someone doesn't want to participate, don't make a fuss about it. At the end of the ceremony, just after the vows, Laura and Jack will light their big unity candle and blow out the two small side candles. Then the four ushers will come forward and light tapers from the unity candle. They'll go back along the center aisle lighting one candle in each row, and the guests will pass the flame along until everyone's candle is glowing."

"Silly nonsense, Laura," her mother muttered.

Laura's face tensed a little.

Kaitlyn pretended not to notice. "After the ceremony, you'll retrieve and extinguish the candles as you show people out. Don't forget it—St. Matthew's may be stone on the outside, but we could still have a nasty fire. And speaking of stone, watch out for the floors. They're slick, and we don't want to have someone in a cast tomorrow. All right, everyone in your places for the processional."

It took several tries to get everyone in the right spot, to get the timing down perfectly, to teach the bridesmaids not to walk too quickly, but to keep their pace steady. Kaitlyn was sick of the sound of the wedding march before she was finished, but finally she had them all in place around the altar, and she went back to the pastor's office to tell him it was his turn.

Her feet were hurting; her blistered heel was burning, and she was beginning to wish that she had skipped glamour and worn her usual slacks suit and the flat shoes that let her dash around the church to demonstrate. She might as well have been comfortable, she thought; she certainly wasn't going to feel fresh by the time she got to the club, anyway. Not with the way this rehearsal was going.

But if every mistake that could be made was taken care of tonight, she thought, maybe it would all go smoothly tomorrow.

She settled into a side row where she could observe while the pastor took over the rehearsal of the ceremony itself. He was affable and understanding, and he must have guided five hundred couples through this rite, Kaitlyn thought. He certainly knew how to put them at ease!

"I won't let any of you make a mistake," he was saying. "Because if you happen to do something unforeseen, we'll just take it from there and fit it in, and it won't be a mistake after all. So you can relax, and—"

Kaitlyn took him at his word. She leaned back a little and slid her three-inch heels off. All she had to do tomorrow was get them to the altar; he'd take it from there.

She let her mind drift as he went on. They'd need another fifteen minutes on the procession, she estimated, then one more run-through of how to get back down the aisle afterward, followed by a few minutes for questions. With any luck, she'd be right on time at the club.

She turned her attention back to the altar just as the pastor said, "Then I'll ask, 'Will you, Laura, take this man to be your lawful husband,' et cetera, and Laura will say—"

Kaitlyn happened to be watching Laura right then, and she saw her pretty face grow slightly paler, and her jaw tense, and her throat work a little as if she suddenly had lost her voice.

Then Laura McCarthy said very clearly, "No."

The single word reverberated through the church and bounced off the lacy arches and the carved friezes and the stone floor. It echoed for a long time, and when it had finished, a frozen hush descended on the assembled group.

Laura put her chin up and looked squarely at her fiancé. "No," she repeated. "I won't."

CHAPTER SEVEN

THERE WAS A NERVOUS LAUGH from the maid of honor, a shrill, hysterical titter that broke off halfway through when the girl clapped her hands over her mouth.

This can't be happening, Kaitlyn thought. Things like this only appear in bad movie scripts. Nobody ever fails to show up at the church. Nobody ever steps forward when the clergyman asks them to speak now or forever hold their peace. And nobody, dammit, ever throws a wrench like this into the rehearsal!

Then she saw the way Laura's fingers were trembling on the spray of plastic flowers that Kaitlyn had given her to use for practice. And not just her fingers, either—the girl's entire body was shaking. She must be ready to hyperventilate, or faint or fly to pieces in a nervous fit.

Kaitlyn started toward her at the same instant that Laura's mother did, but the pastor had recovered his poise even more quickly. "Perhaps this should be resolved in private," he said gently. "Laura and Jack—I'll see you in my study, please. The rest of you will wait right here, I'm sure." The easy cajolery was gone from his voice; it was unmistakably an order.

Laura's mother sank back into the front pew and put her hands over her eyes.

The groom's mother sent a freezing look at her, and said, "I am shocked—I have never seen such ill-mannered behavior in my life!"

"Let's not make things worse, shall we?" Kaitlyn murmured. "If they patch up their differences in there, it wouldn't be pleasant to come back out and find their families at war."

The bridesmaids and ushers were still standing rigidly in line; Kaitlyn urged them out of position and into the sanctuary so they could sit down, at least. It might be minutes, or hours, before that conference in the pastor's study would end. She wondered at what point it would be appropriate for her to knock on the door and find out what was going on. If there wasn't to be a wedding, she might as well send everyone home. But she didn't dare do that without knowing what was happening behind that closed door. The longer they all sat here, the less likely it was that anything would be worked out.

She looked at her wristwatch and sighed. In fifteen minutes she was supposed to meet Marcus and their hosts—the hosts who thought it was such a good idea for an executive to be a married man, because it settled him down and gave his life organization. None of them were going to be pleased about this development.

Well, she thought regretfully, she'd tried to warn Marcus that rehearsals were unpredictable.

She found herself wondering for the first time exactly what that argument between Laura and Jack had been about. The bachelor party, as she had originally thought? Or something else? Was this more than just wedding nerves?

Kaitlyn had half an hour to construct theories, and compile a new list of things to do, just in case—she'd never had to cancel a wedding before. Then she began bracing herself to go and find out what was happening, and she had just stood up to do so when the pastor came out of his office, with Laura beside him and Jack two steps behind.

He paused at the foot of the altar steps and said, "After some discussion, I have concluded that there should be no wedding tomorrow. I wish to make it clear to all of you that this is not a decision made by either Laura or Jack—it is simply that my conscience will not allow me to proceed under these circumstances."

It was just about what Kaitlyn had expected, a cancellation, along with a gentlemanly attempt to ease the blame on the bride and groom.

Jack's mother stood up with a flounce. "Come along, son," she said firmly. "I, for one, never wanted this affair in the first place!"

Jack shook her hand off his arm and stood his ground. For a moment, as he turned to Laura, Kaitlyn held her breath. Would he plead? Apologize? Ask her to reconsider?

"What happened was no big deal," he said. "And you're crazy if you think you're going to hold it over my head and run my life." He stalked down the aisle and out the main door of the church.

Kaitlyn sighed and went back to the pastor's office to call the country club. It was not going to be a pleasant chat with Marcus, she warned herself. But there was nothing else she could do but tell him that she would have to stay with her client.

It was several minutes before Marcus came to the telephone, and after she had explained, there was a timeless span of silence.

Then Marcus said, sounding rather dangerous, "What in the hell do you mean you aren't going to make it to dinner at all? I was just explaining to them that you've been helping out a friend, and that you were unfortunately detained, but you'd be along in a few minutes. What do you expect me to tell them now?"

"For heaven's sake, tell them the truth, Marcus!"

"What truth? That your business is more important to you than your promise to me?"

"Don't twist things. I should think they'd understand that sometimes business interferes with personal lives. Or is that only allowed when it's TurfMaster who benefits?"

"There is no need to be sarcastic, Kaitlyn."

"It's not as if this isn't important—" She stopped suddenly. "Wait a minute. You told them I was just helping out a friend?"

He cleared his throat. "I didn't think it would be well received that you had put your business ahead of mine, Kaitlyn."

"Do you mean to say that you didn't tell them I had a business appointment? You just kept quiet till tonight and then made an excuse for the little woman being late?" Her voice was rising.

"Not exactly, darling—"

"Why didn't you just tell them that I'm not smart enough to start doing my hair on time? That would have been easier! I think we have some things to talk about tomorrow, Marcus."

She slammed the telephone down and stood for a second looking at the diamond ring on her left hand before she went back to the sanctuary. All of a sudden, she felt a little less annoyance, and a bit more empathy, for Laura McCarthy. Whatever was behind the girl's outburst, it must have ripped her apart to actually say it.

Laura was standing by the altar steps. She was alone; the ushers, the bridesmaids, the families—even, apparently, the pastor—were gone. Her head drooped, and she was still clutching the garish spray of plastic flowers, as tightly as if it was actually the beautiful amaryllis bouquet she would have carried tomorrow....

Bouquet, Kaitlyn thought, with a mental snap of the fingers. One more thing that would have to be cancelled. After all the frustration she had gone through about how to make amends for the missing calla lilies...

"You're angry at me too, I suppose," Laura said.

"No—I'm not."

Laura's head came up as if she was startled.

Kaitlyn was a little surprised, herself, to find that she was actually telling the truth, not a socially convenient fiction. "There shouldn't be a wedding unless you're convinced it's the right thing to do," she said quietly. "And you're obviously not convinced. That's all I need to know."

Laura's eyes filled with tears. "I thought you'd gone, too," she whispered. "Are you disgusted with me?"

"Of course not. It's my job to help you."

"My mother left. She refused to help. She said I should at least wait till tomorrow—"

"Before you start canceling things, you mean? She wants to give you a chance to recover your senses, no doubt," Kaitlyn said dryly.

"I won't." Then Laura smiled faintly, for the first time, as she heard what she'd said. "I mean—"

"Well, it certainly wouldn't do her any good to put pressure on you to change your mind now. You brought things to a screeching halt."

"She wanted me to go through with it. And I was going to—especially after what you told me about the attack of nerves everybody has. But when the pastor asked if I would take this man—I just couldn't, Kaitlyn."

"Well, at least you didn't wait till tomorrow," Kaitlyn said practically. "Let's get started. We've got a lot of things to do. I should call the caterer and the florist first, I suppose, and then we'll just start down your invitation list."

The lights began to go off one by one, and the pastor came back to the sanctuary. "Do you need a place to work," he asked, "or to talk? I'll leave you a key—"

Kaitlyn shook her head. "We'll just go over to my house. That's where all the files are, anyway."

Audrey was brewing a cup of tea in the kitchen, which by now looked as if a hurricane had swept through it. She seemed confused when they came in, so Kaitlyn murmured a half explanation as she gave Laura a soft drink, and then ran upstairs to change her clothes.

When she returned Audrey was sitting on the living room couch, with Laura's head in her lap, stroking the girl's hair.

"It is embarrassing to back out like this," Laura was sobbing. "My mother thought I should go through with it, anyway. She says I should just accept the way things are, because all bachelor parties have exotic dancers, and all men do things like that whenever they have the chance."

"Things like what?" Kaitlyn asked almost involuntarily.

Audrey said, dryly, "Didn't she tell you? The condensed version is that the exotic dancer's act would have embarrassed most of the clients of the average bawdy house. And Jack was a willing participant."

"Three days before the wedding," Laura said drearily. "And he's messing around with a—"

"At the country club?" Kaitlyn's voice was practically a screech.

Audrey nodded.

"Well, if that's confirmed," Kaitlyn muttered, "he should be thrown out of the membership. I'll talk to Marcus about it tomorrow."

Then she stopped, suddenly, as she remembered that there were several things she was going to have to talk to Marcus about tomorrow. And before that time came, she was going to have to figure out exactly what she was going to say and do.

At the moment, all she knew was that it wasn't likely to be pleasant.

AT MIDNIGHT they finished calling the out-of-town guests on Laura's list, and decided that there was no more that could be done before morning. Audrey tucked Laura into the extra twin bed in Kaitlyn's room, since the guest room had long since been piled full of boxes, and came back downstairs with a sigh. "As if the fact that he's got a little money makes a man a good husband," she said wearily. "What folly it is to try to manage our children's lives. Whatever mistakes they make only become worse when we try to change their minds." She looked at Kaitlyn, with something in her eyes that was almost fear—as if she'd said more than she had intended—and got up abruptly. "I think I'll make some more tea. Would you like a cup, Kaitlyn?"

Penn was right, Kaitlyn thought unhappily. Mother doesn't like Marcus. She hasn't breathed a word to me, because she doesn't believe in trying to change my mind— or because she thinks that any attempt to influence me would only make things worse. But she's convinced it would be a mistake for me to marry him....

And what about me? she asked herself. *What do I think now?*

She went to bed not quite certain of the answer to that question, and was up again as soon as it was decently light outside. Laura was still asleep in the other twin bed, and though the girl was frowning as if her dreams were tormented ones, Kaitlyn didn't disturb her.

She went downstairs in her terry-cloth bathrobe and bright tartan slippers to telephone the pastor, asking him to post a notice on the church doors because it was obvious that they were not going to be able to reach all the guests before the hour set for the wedding. Kaitlyn decided that she would count herself lucky if she could keep the cake from arriving; she hadn't been able to reach the bakery owner last night. And as for the cartons and cartons of candles that were already standing in the foyer of the church, ready to symbolize the light of new love...

Schnoodle gave a sharp bark from the garden, and Kaitlyn went to let him in. But he was objecting to the presence of a half dozen young men who were coming up the garden path. Around the corner of the house, Kaitlyn could see a rental truck in the driveway.

"We're helping Mrs. Ross move some boxes into storage," one of them explained, and they all trooped past Kaitlyn and into the kitchen before she had even remembered to close her mouth, much less the door.

Audrey hadn't said anything about moving today—had she? Kaitlyn couldn't remember, but that was no sure indication, considering how her week had been going. Half of downtown Springhill could have exploded and burned, and she wouldn't have noticed.

Schnoodle followed the workers in and went straight to his basket, in the one undisturbed corner of the kitchen.

"Some watchdog you are," Kaitlyn told him. Then, hearing her mother in the main hallway starting to give instructions, she shrugged off the whole business and went back to her list.

Within an hour she'd learned to ignore the crew of movers and the steady stream of boxes and furniture that passed through the kitchen and out to the truck. Laura had come down, her voice steadier and her hands no longer trembling after a little sleep, and took over Kaitlyn's place at the telephone. So Kaitlyn was staring out the window at the gradually filling rental truck, wondering how to deal with a cake that would serve three hundred people, when Marcus arrived.

He glanced at the chaos in the kitchen, then said tightly, "I'm shocked, Kaitlyn."

She looked at him for one long moment in which she heard none of the noise that surrounded her, saw none of the confusion. Every iota of her attention was focused on Marcus—at the handsome face with the unyielding expression, and the arrogant set of his shoulders and the cool, assessing look in his eyes.

After what had happened last night, she thought, it was inconceivable that there was not a hint of apology in his voice, or even a bit of caution about approaching this discussion. Surely, even if Marcus believed that she had been mostly at fault, he couldn't have convinced himself that there was nothing at all wrong or shady or unwise about his own actions—could he?

And then Kaitlyn knew exactly how Laura had felt last night, when that weighty question had been asked and the unexpected answer had forced itself from her.

She glanced around the kitchen and shrugged. "I'm afraid you'll have to be more specific than that, Marcus. What's shocking you? Don't you approve of the packing job? Or the fact that Mother isn't using professional movers? Or is it that you couldn't get through on the telephone this morning? Or—"

"Your state of undress, for one thing."

Kaitlyn had forgotten about her robe. It was short and made of summer-weight terry—and now that she thought about it, there had been some glances, ranging from shy to embarrassed to bold, as the young men had passed back and forth through the kitchen.

"Go and put on some clothes this instant."

If he hadn't issued the order, Kaitlyn would have excused herself quietly and gone up to her room. But the cold command set the hair at the back of her neck on end.

"Why?" she asked stubbornly.

"Because we certainly can't get this matter straightened out in the midst of this mess." He looked around with distaste.

"Oh? So at least you're admitting that we've got some things to straighten out?" she asked sweetly. "And you just popped in and expected it to be convenient for me?"

"I certainly couldn't call to arrange an appointment to discuss the problem, could I?"

He was right about that, and Kaitlyn had to admit it.

Laura cupped her hand over the receiver. "I'm sorry, Kaitlyn—I've caused you enough trouble. Look, I don't think there's anything else that you can do. I'll keep calling the guest list, but since there's only one phone line—"

"And since it is your wedding, Laura, and your notion to cancel it," Marcus told her, "it does seem only fair that you do the embarrassing work. Go get dressed, Kaitlyn."

I suppose I might as well, Kaitlyn thought. This discussion would have to be held, and the sooner the better. And he was right, they certainly couldn't talk about it here.

Meekly, she headed for the back stairs.

It was pure stubbornness that made her ignore the sports coat and tie Marcus was wearing and put on ordinary jeans and a pullover cotton sweater. She left her makeup in the case, too, pulled her hair back and captured it with a ribbon at the nape of her neck and shoved her feet into canvas shoes.

When she came back downstairs, Marcus looked momentarily discomfited. "I thought we'd have brunch at the club, but you're hardly dressed for it."

She smiled sweetly. "I'm sorry. I thought you were in a hurry. How about the truck stop instead? You won't be recognized there."

He scowled, and Kaitlyn reminded herself that there was no value to sarcasm at this point. It would be far better to get this talk over with quickly, calmly and without blame. It had all been a mistake, but it was largely she who had made it—and it would not be healed faster by slashing at the wounds.

"I'm sorry, Marcus," she said, with honest regret. "I shouldn't snap at you."

He tucked her solicitously into the front seat of his Mercedes and said, "Of course I understand, darling. It's been a difficult couple of days for you." He went around the car and slid behind the wheel, and playfully shook a finger at her. "I must warn you, though—if you ever hang up a telephone on me again, Kaitlyn, I shall be very unhappy."

"I'm not likely to do that," she murmured.

Marcus smiled. "That's very wise of you."

He took her to the hotel coffee shop, and ordered omelettes for them both. Kaitlyn sat with her elbows propped on the table, her hands wrapped around the hot mug of coffee as if seeking comfort from its warmth, and wondered how to begin. All at once, she felt exhausted, as if the adrenaline that had pumped through her veins, getting her through last night, had suddenly drained away.

"What a hash that girl has made of things," Marcus said.

Kaitlyn contemplated telling him what had really been going on at the noisy bachelor party that had so annoyed him. No, she thought, for not even that would make him sympathetic to Laura. He would probably just be more offended with Jack Bailey—not for his immoral actions, but for daring to interfere with Marcus's peace of mind and the country club's rules.

"Of course, if this episode brings you to your senses, I'll owe her a debt of gratitude."

Kaitlyn took a long swallow from her coffee mug. "What do you mean, if it brings me to my senses?"

"About this business of yours, and the problems it leads to. I suppose now you'll have to sue to collect the rest of the fee you're owed."

Her temper flared. "If you think I'd sue Laura, and add to her pain right now—"

"That's exactly my point, Kaitlyn. You did the work; you've a right to be paid for it, whether there's a wedding or not. But you're too softhearted to go after it. You haven't got the right makeup to be in business, you know—you don't know how to properly organize your time so that you can do more than one thing at once. And you have too much sympathy for people to be a good manager."

"Are you saying I have no killer instinct?" She raised her cup to her lips and looked at him over the rim of it.

"That's perhaps wording it a little strongly, but—"

"Well, I'm proud that I'm not some sort of shark. And I don't have any intention of ever trying to become one, either. My business is service, Marcus—" And, she reminded herself, there was no point in carrying this any further, because the business was not really what they came here to talk about. "Marcus," she said more gently. "I was very hurt last night when you pretended to your colleagues that my business didn't even exist."

"Kaitlyn—"

"I know you were trying to make a good impression on them, but it didn't work out that way at all, did it? You made me look like some kind of thoughtless, brainless female instead." She drew a deep breath. "I admit it was inefficient to book myself two appointments at the same time, but it was an oversight, that's all. Would you honestly rather have them think I was just being rude for the fun of it?"

He sighed. "Well, of course, when you put it that way—but if it wasn't for the damned business, Kaitlyn, there wouldn't have been a problem!"

She looked at him for a long moment, and then she said quietly, "My business is not the problem, Marcus. We have a basic disagreement about what we want out of life—*that's* the problem." She twisted the engagement ring from her finger and held it out to him, the marquise diamond sparkling subtly in the sunshine that flooded the coffee shop.

He didn't reach for it. "Don't be melodramatic, Kaitlyn," he said briskly. "Breaking off an engagement is a very serious matter."

"I'm quite aware of that."

"And it's a very poor device for getting attention."

"I'm dead serious, Marcus. Please show enough respect for me to believe that I'm not doing this lightly." Kaitlyn's arm was already a bit weary, stretched out at full length across the table. The ring seemed to weigh a full pound.

He didn't move. "Just because Laura backed out of her wedding is certainly no reason for you to have some sort of sympathy pains and do the same thing."

"Marcus, take the blasted ring."

"No," he said firmly. "You're tired and you're angry, and I admit that perhaps I should have been more cautious last night. But hurt feelings are no reason for breaking off our engagement, Kaitlyn.''

"Yes, they are. Precisely because you don't understand how important hurt feelings can be." She dropped the ring in the ashtray in the center of the table and stood up just as the waitress brought two plates, each half covered by a still-sizzling omelette. She had a momentary urge to sit down and dig in; the food looked good, and suddenly, with the worst behind her, she felt almost hungry. Then she thought better of it. "If you'll excuse me, I'm moving this afternoon. I'd better go start getting organized."

The way the words popped out surprised her a bit, for she hadn't really thought about it till that moment. It made sense, however; her afternoon was suddenly free, and when those young men were finished with her mother's things, one more load would have all of Kaitlyn's moved, as well. It would be a great deal easier than trying to do it herself, tomorrow.

"We aren't finished discussing this."

"Yes, we are." She stepped toward the door.

Marcus wiped his lips with his napkin—ever proper, Kaitlyn noted—scooped up the ring from the ashtray and followed her.

"You're distraught, Kaitlyn. You can't possibly make reasonable decisions in the heat of anger."

"He may not call you Kitten," Penn had said, *"but he treats you like one...."* Well, Kaitlyn thought, as infuriating as Penn was, he'd certainly been right about that much.

She pulled her car keys from the side pocket of her handbag and then remembered that she didn't have her car. She said idly, "Where would you have taken me for a honeymoon, Marcus?"

He blinked, looking a bit owlish. "Does it make a difference?"

"You mean, if I like the destination will I change my mind? No. I was just curious."

"I've always liked the idea of Bermuda," he said stiffly.

"February in Bermuda," she mused. She dropped the keys back into her handbag. "Careful, Marcus. The waitress is ready to call the law on you for leaving without paying your bill." She pushed the door open.

"I won't stand for being treated in this high-handed way," he warned. "If you walk out now, Kaitlyn, it's over."

"That's the general idea." She said it as gently as she could, and she honestly felt sorry for him when she realized that the look in his eyes wasn't anger, or resentment. It was simple confusion.

Tired as she was, she could feel a new spring come into her step as she left the central business district and walked toward the residential section of town. If that was what Marcus called "discussing a problem," she thought, she was grateful she wasn't going to be discussing any more of them with him.

DARKNESS ALWAYS SEEMED to come earlier and more suddenly at Sapphire Lake than in town, because of the hills and the trees that shielded the little valley. By the time the last of Kaitlyn's boxes were carried into Jill's cabin and the movers left, dusk was starting to settle over the peaceful water.

She looked around with a sinking heart. Stacks of cartons occupied every corner of the main room of the A-frame cabin, and though from her position at the bottom of the spiral stairs she couldn't see into the single bedroom up in the loft, she knew it was piled high, as well.

Her car was still packed full of clothes. Paper bags of supplies filled the small table in the tiny galley kitchen at the back of the cabin; she had shoved the perishables into the refrigerator, but she would have to sort the rest out before she could even fix herself a peanut-butter sandwich. There was a bed to be made, if she could find sheets—either among her own possessions, or somewhere in a closet. Preferably her own, she thought, because the whole cabin felt damp and chilly, as if it had been closed up too long. A fire might banish that musty feeling—if she only had the energy to go looking for wood and kindling. But she didn't, so she'd just have to settle down to work and at least get enough done so she could crawl into a comfortable bed. Tomorrow would be enough time for luxuries.

She flipped the switch to turn on the electric lantern that hung in the center of the big room. The bulb flared into unnatural brilliance for a fraction of a second, and then popped ominously and went dark again. Kaitlyn swore under her breath. The damned lantern was her main source of light. It was also too high to reach—twelve feet off the floor if it was an inch—and she couldn't remember seeing a ladder or a step stool anywhere. Now, in the rapidly gathering dark, she couldn't even look for one, or for a replacement bulb, either. And it was a sure thing that she couldn't do much unpacking without light.

"I should have picked up a box of Laura's candles," she muttered. "She certainly isn't ever going to use them all."

She chewed on her lower lip for a moment and then took Schnoodle's leash down from the hook by the back door and fastened it to his collar. She might as well kill two birds with one stone—she could walk the dog as well as check the neighborhood for a ladder.

She paused on the gravel path just outside the A-frame and then forced herself to turn toward the Caldwell cabin. It would be only sensible to ask Penn first, since his was the nearest cabin she knew was occupied. It would look very strange if she didn't.

She hadn't exactly planned to go calling on him, and certainly not so soon. It would be much better to be casual about it, she had decided, and then when he inevitably found out that she was living in the cabin—well, she'd take it from there. But she certainly couldn't function in the dark.

With any luck at all, she decided, Penn would be out, and she could go on down the row of cabins until she found someone else at home.

But there was a car in the driveway, as well as the beat-up old pickup truck. It was not a new car, or a luxurious one, but it was nice enough, and the unmistakable smell of a steak searing on a barbecue grill drifted across the path.

He's entertaining, she thought. That's just great; it would look as if nosy Kaitlyn couldn't stand not knowing who was visiting him!

She walked slowly around the corner of the house. Schnoodle began tugging at his leash and every muscle of his body went tight and alert as he sniffed the air.

There was no one on the big deck, though the barbecue was certainly at work; she could see an occasional puff of smoke and hear the sizzle of fat dripping onto the hot coals. She stopped and looked around, down to the sandy beach and the lakeshore, lit only by the occasional glow of fireflies.

Perhaps he wasn't entertaining, after all, she thought, or else he was doing so inside. Despite her best intentions of minding her own business, Kaitlyn looked up at the sleeping porch, which was cantilevered out over part of the deck. It, too, was dark.

"What brings you out here?" said a lazy voice from behind her. Kaitlyn spun around, and Schnoodle excitedly pulled her toward the mulberry tree beside the house.

A big rope hammock was strung from the trunk of the huge old tree, with the other end anchored to the deck rail, and in it lay Penn. His feet were crossed at the ankle and his hands were folded behind his head.

"Hi," she said. Her voice was little more than a squeak.

Great line, she told herself ironically. How original. Just the way she had sounded when she was sixteen and trying to make an impression on him in the lunch line—the day she'd dropped her tray of tuna casserole on his toe.

Well, these were not the old days, she reminded herself.

And that was part of the problem, she thought. For she wanted those old days back again—the days when it had seemed perpetual summer.

The days when Penn was the center of her life.

CHAPTER EIGHT

MORE FOOL YOU if that's the truth! she told herself unsympathetically. Longing for those lazy days of summer was simply asking for a repetition of that awful hurt she'd felt because, though Penn had been the center of her life, she had never been the center of his.

No, she reflected. She didn't truly want anything of the sort. This was only an attack of general nostalgia; it must have been building for weeks, brought on by the sale of the house she'd grown up in, and compounded by exhaustion and tension and hunger and a touch of uncertainty about where her future lay, now that Marcus was no longer in it.

Don't let yourself get maudlin about how wonderful things used to be, she ordered herself. It was easy to look back and see only the good. And even more important, she shouldn't let herself be overcome by the difficulties she faced at the moment and start thinking that Penn had anything to do with this sudden attack of loneliness. Because he didn't.

"Are we playing charades?" he asked with a note in his voice that was almost exasperation. "Sorry, but it's a bit too dark for it, Kitten."

She grasped at the reminder with relief. "That's my problem exactly," she said. "I'm looking for a hundred-watt light bulb and a ladder of some kind so I can install it. It's awfully dark at the moment over at Jill's cabin."

"Let me think where we might find one." He closed his eyes. To all appearances he was asleep.

"Don't think too hard," she said, with a tinge of irony. "I wouldn't want to burn out your brain. If it's too much trouble to find a ladder, a grappling hook might work; I can try to snag the lantern chain from the loft."

Penn didn't react to the gibe. "I've got it. The ladder's in the toolshed." He rolled out of the hammock in one easy, catlike motion. "I'll bring it over. It's too heavy for you."

He not only delivered the ladder but installed a new light bulb, as well, and when it blinked into life he sat down on the top rung and looked around. Even the high-wattage bulb didn't send light into every inch of the big room—the small nooks and corners still had an intimate dimness—but it was ample to see the mess, and Penn examined it with interest.

"We'll be neighbors for a while," Kaitlyn said, trying to make it sound careless. "Just until I can find a place in town."

He didn't answer, and she moved back to the kitchenette and started to unpack the bags of food. He seemed in no hurry to leave.

Finally Kaitlyn said, "Don't forget your steak. It smelled too good to let it burn to a crisp." Her mouth was watering just thinking about it, and with determination she rummaged till she found the jar of peanut butter.

He glanced at his wristwatch. "It should be perfect in three more minutes." He eyed the peanut butter and added, "There's more than enough—come on over, if you like."

Kaitlyn didn't look at him. "I wasn't hinting."

"I know." He folded up the ladder and carried it out, whistling.

She fought a very brief battle with her conscience and lost, because the breathtaking aroma of that steak seemed to have wafted all the way down the lane and through her windows. So she followed him, bracing herself when she rounded the corner of the Caldwell cabin for whatever pointed remark he might make.

But Penn only smiled, gave her a plate and waved a hand at the barbecue, where an enormous sirloin still sizzled gently. It had been neatly cut in half.

"I thought you had a guest," she said.

He looked around as if to make sure. "Just me."

"You're a two-vehicle person?"

"No. The truck's borrowed."

"Oh. Well, you're right about having plenty of food," she muttered.

Penn shrugged. "It's a nuisance to light the coals, so I've been cooking in quantity and then warming up the leftovers in the microwave the next day."

"Warming up a steak in the—Penn, you cretin, it's an indignity to zap a beautiful piece of meat in a microwave." Then, too late, she remembered that it wasn't prudent to insult her host.

Penn only shrugged. "See what horrors you've saved me from by eating half my dinner?" he asked mildly. "Would you like a beer? Soft drink? Lake water?"

She chose the beer, and he opened a bottle and handed it to her. "I thought you had a wedding to manage this afternoon."

"Don't remind me." She sliced off a bite of her steak and savored it. "You're a jinx, Penn."

"Now wait a minute," he protested. "I saved you—"

"Yes, and then warned me about protecting myself from tornadoes and other acts of God."

Penn eyed the sky, which was perfectly clear. The evening star had appeared, hanging low over the pine trees at the horizon. "Your wedding got hit by a tornado?" he asked warily.

"Slightly different kind of tornado, but just as damaging."

He fed a scrap of meat to Schnoodle, who had been abasing himself on the deck, his nose quivering. The animal snapped up the treat and watched eagerly as Penn cut the next bite.

"You're teaching him bad habits," Kaitlyn warned. "It isn't good for his teeth."

"I feel sorry for the poor fellow. I've never seen him on a leash before."

"It's just until he finds his way about and learns his limits. He's getting to be half blind, you know, and I wouldn't want him to fall in the lake. Besides, if I took the leash off right now, he'd think he belonged here." She sliced her baked potato open. "You're absolutely certain you don't want a dog? If you're going to be in Springhill for a few months while you build a house—"

For a moment, she thought he hadn't heard. Then he said almost absently, "I knew I should have kept my mouth shut till the deal was firm."

The breath caught in her throat, and she almost choked on a bite of lettuce. If he didn't buy the Delaney place, he wouldn't have a place to build a house in Springhill, and so he wouldn't stay here at all. It was relief she was feeling; it must have been.

"You mean it isn't firm?" she managed to say, after a moment. "You certainly made it sound as if it was all signed and delivered."

"Last-minute problems." But he obviously didn't want to discuss them, for he asked instead, "What happened to your wedding, anyway?"

"Last-minute problems," she repeated wryly, then told him about the bachelor party. She was annoyed when his only response was laughter.

"All right," she said irritably. "Call me a prude if you want, but I consider that to be ample grounds for breaking off an engagement. I suppose you think Laura's mother was right? If you tell me that all bachelor parties have strippers or dancers or bimbos jumping out of cakes, Penn, and all men grab that sort of opportunity whenever it's presented, and so Laura should just have shrugged it off—"

"Now, wait a minute. I didn't say that. It's a bit insulting to the entire species of men to lump them all together in a category, wouldn't you say?"

"I'd call them a subspecies, if that's the way they all behave."

"Oh, not all of them, certainly. I'm sure you don't have anything to worry about with Marcus."

The earnest reassurance in his voice made Kaitlyn want to hit him over the head with the remainder of her steak. He didn't have to imply that there was anything *wrong* with Marcus, for heaven's sake!

"Still," Penn mused, "I don't think Jack Bailey got what he deserved."

She set her plate aside and leaned froward. "All right, perhaps I'm naive. But if you're honestly suggesting that Laura should have simply put up with that sort of behavior—"

"Oh, no. If Jack still has a juvenile fascination with exotic dancers, she was wise to get rid of him. But if she had asked me, I'd have suggested she wait till today. She could have simply explained at the altar in front of their assembled guests why she wasn't interested in continuing the ceremony.''

Kaitlyn gasped.

"Just think of it," Penn said earnestly. "It would have been far more entertaining than the average wedding. Besides, if she'd done it my way, all that work and money wouldn't have gone for nothing. She would at least have had the party, to celebrate her return to sanity and the single life.''

Kaitlyn gathered up her plate and beer glass and stalked into the kitchen, letting the screen door slam behind her. "Don't you have any sympathy for anyone?" she asked when she heard him come in. She didn't turn around; she was swishing hot water and detergent into a foam in the sink as if her life depended on getting the best possible bubbles.

"Of course I do." He sounded surprised. "I just don't see the benefit of crying into my beer tonight because Laura is unhappy.''

She had to admit the sense in that, but the episode still annoyed her, and she scrubbed the dishes with more than the necessary force. Why did he seem to have to turn everything into a joke?

It is not your problem, Kaitlyn, she reminded herself.

He started a pot of coffee and then dried the dishes, and by the time everything was cleaned up the scent of the brew was drifting through the kitchen. Kaitlyn carried her cup toward the deck, and stopped beside the kitchen table, which was heaped with papers. Sketches, she guessed, and floor plans, and without thinking she reached for the top one to take a closer look.

Penn turned from the refrigerator, where he was putting away the last of the food, and stood watching her with his hands planted firmly on his hips.

Kaitlyn looked up, belatedly feeling the weight of his gaze. "Oh. I'm sorry. This is private stuff, I suppose." She put the sheet back carefully on top of the stack, but she couldn't stop herself from saying, once they were out on the deck, "That isn't the house you were planning to build on the Delaney place, is it?"

He shot a suspicious look at her. "Who said anything about the Delaney place?"

"Oh, come on, Penn. It's no secret that's the piece of property you're dealing on; you said yourself this town doesn't need a newspaper."

"Granted. But why don't you think it's an actual house I plan to build?" He'd stopped halfway across the deck, and he stood there, very still. "Or do you think I make it all up as I go along? Pick up a board and then decide where to nail it?"

She giggled a little. "Sort of like playing the piano by ear? Not at all; of course you have a plan. But you can't mean to plant that elaborate house on that trashy lot. It will never sell."

He came across to lean against the deck rail beside her. "That lot may be trashy at the moment, but it doesn't have to stay that way. And it's right on the edge of a very good neighborhood."

"With only an impassible ravine dividing them," she scoffed. "It will never work."

"Perhaps you're right." But he didn't sound particularly interested in whether she was or not, and so Kaitlyn fell silent. It wasn't her business, after all, no matter what he built—or where.

The full moon was rising above the horizon, orange gold and brilliant, its reflection wavering slightly in the still lake. It looked as though the water was the surface of an antique mirror, ever so slightly concave here and convex there, throwing irregularities into the image. The light sent mammoth shadows creeping across the beach and the paths and the cabins.

The silent drama of moonrise on the lake had always had the power to catch at Kaitlyn's throat with its sheer perfect beauty, whether she was watching it from a canoe out on the water, or from a blanket on the beach, or from the deck of the Caldwell cabin, with Penn's arm around her—

She turned her head a little, and her breath began to come more quickly, in tiny, almost painful gasps. No, it was not her imagination. It had been so natural—the way he'd moved closer, the gentle brush of his arm around her shoulders—that she hadn't even been aware of his touch for a moment or two. But she was standing in the circle of his arm, a mere heartbeat away from him. If she wanted him to kiss her, all she had to do was raise her face to his.

Don't be a fool, she told herself. But then a question rose from the back of her brain: why shouldn't she enjoy the moment? The moon, the beautiful night, the quiet lake, a man and a woman—all the proper ingredients. And though there was not and never again could be anything between them, there was no reason not to indulge in a simple kiss.

His mouth was tender, warm, mobile, gentle. It was a soft kiss, without a hint of force or domination, and equally lacking any hint of pleading or begging. It was as if he was confident that she had made her choice as freely as he had, and that she was enjoying this in very much the same way—without compulsion or fear, and without promises or guarantees. . . .

It was then that she recognized the wave of feeling that had come over her when she'd realized that he might not stay in Springhill, after all. It had not been relief, as she'd thought it was. It had been fear, instead—a fear so deep-seated that she hadn't recognized it, and so strong that it was just short of panic. Fear at the idea of losing him once more.

She'd tried for ten years to tell herself that Penn no longer mattered; she'd come very close to believing it. She'd put her life back together after he had rejected her, and she'd found someone else to love. But it had all been pretense. Even on the night when Marcus had proposed to her, she had known, deep inside her heart, that it was false; that was why she'd hesitated instead of giving him an answer.

The reassuring tale she had created for herself had been just like the tissue-paper wrapping on a gift. As long as one didn't look too closely, a single layer of tissue could hide a lot. But once it was subjected to inspection, its power of concealment melted away, and the contents lay plainly— and sometimes unpleasantly—in view.

For there was no denying, now, that she still loved Penn—and that she had wasted all the effort she had spent over the years in convincing herself that she did not.

She drew away from him awkwardly, almost with a jerk.

"Scared?" he whispered.

He sounded ever so slightly off balance, as if things had gone just a little beyond what he had intended, as if he had stepped just a fraction of an inch beyond some predetermined line of safety.

And that was the second unpleasant truth, which lay open to her now. It was a truth that was as undeniable as if it had been a rattlesnake curled at her feet, this knowledge that she was no more important to Penn now than she had ever been.

If he had cared about her at all, it would have mattered to him that she was going to marry Marcus. But it obviously didn't, or he wouldn't dream up gifts, or tease about her wedding night or volunteer to manage her reception.

And now that she wasn't going to marry Marcus—what was Penn likely to think of that?

Nothing at all, she realized. He'd simply shrug and make some sort of joke of that, too.

And that, she told herself drearily, *will truly break my heart.*

SHE MADE HER ESCAPE with the excuse of being tired, and refused his offer to walk her back to Jill's cabin. It was only a step away, she told him without looking up, and she had the dog; Schnoodle might not be much protection, but he certainly would warn her if anything was amiss. Besides, Penn could see the cabin lights come on and be assured that she was fine.

He didn't argue about it, and she went off alone, with Schnoodle's leash wrapped around her wrist.

He's probably glad that I'm not going to be the clinging-vine kind of neighbor, Kaitlyn told herself. Borrowing ladders and light bulbs was one thing, but insisting on being walked home and watched over and protected would quickly get to be a nuisance.

Her rubber-soled shoes crunched in the gravel on the old path. It brought back with unbearable clarity the memory of another moonlit night when she had left the Caldwell cabin alone, well after dark. But that night she had been running, chased not by wild animals but by the demons in her own mind....

She turned the cabin lights on. What was a reasonable length of time to leave them burning, she wondered, so that it would appear she had settled down for the night? She certainly didn't want Penn to think she was too agitated to sleep. Or, conversely, that she was sitting alone in the dark, just thinking.

Then she snapped the lights off firmly. Penn wouldn't be watching, she told herself bluntly. If she seriously believed that he was likely to sit over there observing her every move and trying to figure out what she was thinking—well, that was just one more symptom of her obsession. And she had better get rid of it right away, for the sake of her mental health.

She curled up on the couch before the empty fireplace, her feet up, her fingers half-consciously stroking Schnoodle's soft fur. She watched the moonlight creep across the room and allowed herself to reconstruct that other moonlit night, so long ago now. It was a memory that still had the power to wound her, and she had long since buried it deep in the back corners of her mind. She had hidden it away so well that it was not easy any more to dredge up the details of a time when the easy, lazy promise of summer had been abruptly torn away from them all....

It had been almost a month after the Caldwells' accident before Penn's awful cough had finally gone away— the hoarse aftermath of all the fuel-polluted lake water that had choked him in the minutes after the collision. By then the visible bruises had healed, as well, and his friends were beginning to try to get things back to normal. They went about it rather awkwardly sometimes, and the first time Kaitlyn had heard the old half-serious insults directed at Penn she'd been shocked and frightened. But that was when he'd finally started to laugh again. His laughter had seemed forced sometimes, but it was certainly a sign that he was healing, that one day he would be well. She seized on it with gratitude.

She spent all the time with him that she could, and her parents, though concerned about her single-mindedness, were understanding. When Penn abruptly decided that the house in town held too many ghosts to let him rest, and moved up to the Caldwells' lake house, Audrey Ross had rented a cabin and taken Kaitlyn up, as well. Audrey had mothered Penn as best she could—as much as he would allow her to—and she had never known about the many nights when Kaitlyn slipped over the balcony rail and went back down the gravel path to the Caldwell cabin, where Penn waited for her under the big old mulberry tree.

Even if Audrey had known, Kaitlyn thought, there was nothing in those midnight expeditions to frighten her. They had been innocent enough, that was certain. The two of them would walk along the lakeshore until Penn was exhausted enough to sleep a little. Or they would just sit together, sometimes talking and sometimes not.

They had never discussed the accident itself. Penn veered away from the subject whenever it came too near, and Kaitlyn hadn't pressed for the details, or for his feelings. It was best to let him forget, she thought. And he would forget in time; he was already better. With the inexperience and the optimism of her youth, she was convinced of it.

And so she was terrified one night when he wasn't waiting under the mulberry tree, and she found him inside the cabin with his mother's collection of pretty pebbles— picked up on her walks around the lake—spread out on the hearth. He was sitting as if he was made of stone, as well, and in the harshness of his grief he didn't even hear her come in.

When finally she managed to reach him and break through that silent stillness, he had turned to her for solace, and there had been no question in her mind about the rightness of what she offered him. She loved him; someday soon she would marry him. And if in the meantime there was comfort for him in her body—in knowing how deeply he was loved—well, what could be so wrong about that? It would be cruel to turn away when he needed her so badly.

And so she'd made love with him. The experience was not exactly the culmination of her dreams and expectations—but perhaps, she told herself, it was the dreams and expectations that were at fault. And afterward, when she'd cradled him close and stroked his damp hair back from his brow and said something—lost now in the dim reaches of memory—about how much she loved him, it had been a stunning shock when he had pulled away from her as if he couldn't bear to be touched.

"No," he said hoarsely. "I think I've lost my mind."

The words would be forever engraved on her heart, along with the way he'd looked at her—as if he'd never quite seen her before.

She had tried to pull him back, to comfort him. But he'd acted as if her touch was sandpaper, and had started to talk, almost to himself. It should not have happened, he said. It had all been a horrible mistake—

She remembered feeling a momentary consolation that even in the midst of his pain he felt so bad about taking advantage of her—of breaking the rules they had set up for themselves. She'd tried to reassure him, to remind him that he hadn't forced her, that it had been her own choice, after all.

What if there was to be a baby, he had asked, and added that he suspected that she had already considered that possibility.

Not quite certain of what he meant, feeling uneasy and almost as if she were under attack, Kaitlyn had told him that she hadn't been thinking quite that clearly. But in any case, what did it matter? They would be married soon, anyway—

Those few words, to her unutterable astonishment, had been like tinder set to dynamite. She'd hardly recognized him—the Penn she loved—in the man who'd told her coldly that only a terrible lapse in his judgment could have allowed her to manipulate him into such a position—where a pregnancy might force him into an unwanted marriage.

Manipulate—force—unwanted. The words had rained down on her like knives, slicing her heart, her self-esteem, her love into tiny oozing fragments. And she had run from him, pounding back along the gravel paths as if the hounds of hell were at her heels.

Even the horrible accident that had swept Penn's parents away hadn't stripped Kaitlyn of the primary illusion of youth—the sense that the world was essentially a fair place, and that good intentions would be rewarded. But that night had ripped her innocence from her, and taught her cynicism instead.

She had crept back into the Ross cabin and lain awake for most of the night. In the days that followed, she hadn't gone out of her way to avoid Penn entirely—to do so would cause too many questions—but she had steadfastly refused to look at him, to talk to him, to listen. Not, she reminded herself, that he had made much of an effort to talk to her, either. He had certainly not apologized, and when she had told him that there was no further fear of pregnancy he'd been unable to hide his relief. She'd almost hated him, then.

She told her parents only that the accident had changed Penn into a person she no longer knew; and despite her steadfast refusal to answer questions, she thought they were almost relieved to find that she was quietly getting on with her life. It was too late to change her plans to attend the university Penn had chosen, but it was a big place. There would be no difficulty in avoiding him, she assured herself.

But that, it turned out, had been an unnecessary worry. For Penn hadn't gone back to school at all. Just weeks before the fall term was to start, he'd packed a duffel bag and left Springhill, asking his parents' attorney to close up the cabin on the lake and to sell everything else.

Springhill had talked, of course—at length—about psychic wounds and irresponsibility and adolescent reactions and the shame it all was. And then some other minor scandal had come to light, and Penn Caldwell was all but forgotten.

Except for the occasional postcard from some exotic place and the occasional reminder in casual conversation. And except for Kaitlyn—who could never forget the harshness of what that night had told her—that he felt no love for her, or any desire for permanence or commitment. That he saw her as a hunter who wanted only to capture him, no matter what means were necessary. That the possibility of her having his child was a weapon held to his head....

She put her face down into the cushion of the couch, and a single sob, harsh and painful, escaped her, followed by a hot flow of tears that for all these years she had been too angry to shed.

He'd been right, she thought, that afternoon at the ice-cream shop, when he'd accused her of still being angry at him because he hadn't wanted to marry her. She had suppressed it well—until now.

The moon was at its zenith by the time her tears stopped, and the light that had earlier cascaded through the windows had now shrunk to small uneven squares on the hardwood floor. Her legs felt stiff from the long spell of sitting in one position; her body ached as if she had unconsciously been tensing every muscle.

But there was some degree of peace in her heart. She'd finally taken out this memory and shaken it free of dust and grime and given it a close inspection. And now, with the wisdom that came inevitably with a few more years of living, she could see things differently. She could even forgive Penn for what had happened. She could understand, now, that in the stress of the moment he'd been hardly aware of what he was doing that night. They'd been caught, the two of them, in the midst of forces they couldn't understand.

And though she knew that every word he'd said that night had been the truth, she also knew that it was not truly Penn who had said those hurtful things. It had been some new person, a hard and angry one who had been forged in the pain of that searing explosion. It hadn't been the gentle Penn she had loved—the one she could still see inside the man he'd become.

The one who, despite everything, she still loved.

There was a strange sense of serenity that came from admitting it, of facing the truth at long last.

"And just where does that get you, Kaitlyn Ross?" she asked herself wearily. "Right back to the beginning, I'd say. With nowhere left to go."

CHAPTER NINE

IT TOOK KAITLYN most of the night to talk herself back to common sense, to convince herself that loving Penn made no real difference at all. The fact that she'd realized what had happened to her and faced up to it didn't change the underlying truth. So her painful admission that she still loved him shouldn't upset her world. The best thing to do would be to put it out of her mind again and go on about her business as usual.

She told herself that as she brushed her teeth. She repeated it as she ate her cold cereal. She hammered it into her conscious mind as she unpacked a half dozen boxes.

And as she went out to her car to begin carrying in her clothing, and saw him at the edge of the beach, his arm upraised in the instant before he cast a fishing line into the water, she knew that all the self-lecturing had been in vain. No matter how sensible she tried to be, it wasn't going to work. The realization that she loved him, after all—despite everything—had changed her world forever.

He must have heard her, for he waved. Then he turned casually back to his fishing. But that was all it took to destroy her carefully constructed logic. Kaitlyn's heart seemed to turn over, and she grabbed an armful of clothes at random from her car and hurried back inside with them, as breathless as if she had just finished a marathon.

You're being a fool, she told herself. *You're no longer a girl with stardust in your eyes. We are both different people than we were ten years ago.*

And that was part of the problem. For there was something about this new Penn that touched her heart more than ever. There was something about him now—some deep reserve, some essential aloneness, some quiet space that no one could quite reach—which had been created as the wounds from his loss had healed. And that silent mystery attracted her, and threatened her peace of mind, as nothing else ever had.

She had loved him then, as much as she had known it was possible to love. But now—now she loved him more.

When she went out to her car again he was gone from the lakeshore, and she didn't see a trace of him for the rest of the day. The message, she thought, was obvious. He could have called a greeting; he could have come up the hill to say hello or to offer her a hand. But he hadn't. And so the most sensible response was for her to be just as casual—as neighborly—as friendly. There would be conversations over the back fence, there would be help offered and accepted—but they would essentially go their own ways, as all good neighbors did.

And that was what she wanted, she told herself. She would be a fool to let herself be drawn back into that whirlpool of attraction. She knew very well that there was no future in it.

But that knowledge, and the resolution to guard herself carefully, didn't make her feel much better.

On Monday afternoon, she stopped at Stephanie's office to pick up the final papers on the sale of the house; Audrey had gone to stay with her sister as soon as the movers had finished work, and Kaitlyn had promised to take the check to the bank for her. Stephanie was still at the closing but was due back any minute, the secretary said, and showed Kaitlyn into the private office.

Kaitlyn wasn't nosy by nature; besides, there was never anything confidential left lying around Stephanie's desk. There was, however, always plenty to look at: a fresh red rose in a crystal vase, new photographs of Stephanie's husband and two children, and a wall full of certificates and licenses relating to her profession. Today there was also a coffee mug that proclaimed Selling Land Is A Dirty Business and—leaning against the wall in the corner, as if Stephanie was still thinking about a place to hang it—a framed watercolor of a house. It was a very nice piece of art, and a very nice house—a contemporary, upscale structure that looked as light and airy as a gossamer web and yet substantial enough to withstand wind or hail or blizzard.

Kaitlyn was still studying it when Stephanie breezed in and dropped into her chair with a moan. "I hate closings," she said. "They always hit a snag. Nice house, don't you think?"

"I haven't seen it, have I? The real house, I mean. Nobody around here is building things like this."

"Not yet," Stephanie said cheerfully. She extracted Audrey's check from her portfolio and handed it across the desk with a flourish. "But soon—if I can just get the Delaney deal put together."

Kaitlyn took the slip of paper absentmindedly; she was still looking at the water color instead. "You don't mean—that can't be the house Penn is going to build?"

"Oh, no. This particular one is in Georgia. I've only got it as a sample of his work. But most of his designs have that same luscious feel to them, as if the houses need to be anchored to bedrock to keep them from floating away."

"But I thought—" Kaitlyn stopped, and tried again. "You said *Penn's* designs? Do you mean he drew this himself? All of it?"

Stephanie looked at her rather oddly, and when she spoke it was as if she was talking to a child. "That's generally what architects do, Kaitlyn. He went back to school several years ago and finished his degree."

Kaitlyn could feel the color draining out of her face.

Stephanie sighed. "Don't expect me to believe you haven't heard that."

"Well, it's true. Nobody told me," Kaitlyn said stiffly.

"No one told you? Or you weren't listening, because it didn't fit with what you wanted to think of Penn?" Stephanie's tone was softer, more understanding, than her words.

"But then why is he driving nails himself?" Kaitlyn picked up the watercolor. Her hands were almost shaking. "If he can do things like this—"

"Why don't you ask him?" Stephanie said imperturbably. "When do you want to look at apartments, Kaitlyn? The end of the week is good for me."

Kaitlyn drove back along the twisting roads toward Sapphire Lake with her mind only halfway on the business at hand. "And I thought the drawing I saw on the kitchen table that night must have been a stock floor plan he picked up somewhere," she muttered. "It never occurred to me that Penn could do anything of this sort. I wonder what else he does?"

"Why don't you ask him?" Stephanie had blithely suggested, but that was easy for her to say. It was different for Kaitlyn.

"It's different," she admitted, "because she's right, dammit. I've gone about with a chip on my shoulder where he's concerned—expecting the worst, almost *wanting* the worst because it helped to soothe my wounded pride. And now—"

Now, was it too late to change things? And did she even want to try to change them, or would that only make it more difficult for her in the long run?

Penn was on the beach again with his fishing gear when she got back to the lake. Today he was wearing cutoff jeans and nothing else. From a hundred yards away she could see the ripple of muscles in his shoulders as he sent the line spinning out into the water in a long, smooth cast, and she shivered a little and hurried into the house.

But she couldn't concentrate on addressing Kathy Warren's invitations, and after she ruined the second vellum envelope she put the project aside. There were too many questions in her mind, and her conscience was nagging at her.

She wasn't normally the sort of person who held grudges, or who went around hurling accusations and telling others what was wrong with them. The provocation to tell Penn what she thought of him had been extreme that afternoon in the ice-cream shop, or she never would have let loose her private opinions. At the least, she owed it to Penn to let him know that she had discovered her error—and that she was sorry.

And that's all it needs to be, she told herself. A dignified apology.

So she fixed two glasses of iced tea and carried them down to the shore and climbed onto the big flat rock at the water's edge. "How's the fishing?" she asked.

"Fair." Penn gulped the drink almost greedily. "I wish I'd brought along my spear, though."

"Spear? As in spearfishing?"

"It takes a certain knack, but once you learn how to do it, it's actually easier than using a line. Besides, the fish in this lake wouldn't be expecting it."

"Isn't spearfishing illegal?" Kaitlyn asked doubtfully.

"That's why they wouldn't be expecting it." He didn't sound concerned.

Kaitlyn sipped her tea and said carefully, "Penn, why did you let me go on thinking that you'd never finished school?"

The sunshine glimmering off the water's surface seemed to bother him all of a sudden, for the corners of his eyes crinkled up and he frowned a little. She knew he had heard her; there was no sound on the quiet lake shore to drown out her words. But for a long moment it seemed that he was going to pretend deafness.

Well, she thought stubbornly, *I can wait just as long as he can.*

He shrugged. "Because it didn't matter."

Kaitlyn swallowed an ice cube. The jagged edge seemed to tear her throat, hurting all the way down—but that pain wasn't as bad as the pain his comment had caused.

That puts you squarely in your place, she told herself. *"It didn't matter."* He might as well have said, What you think of me isn't important, Kaitlyn, because you don't matter an ounce to me....

Well, that's nothing new, she thought flatly. She should have expected him to say something like that.

"So what's brought it up now, Kaitlyn? Are the letters after my name so important to you?"

"No," she said slowly. "I wish you'd told me, that's all. I don't like looking like a fool."

He darted a glance at her and turned back to the water, without any indication of a desire to answer.

"Obviously whether I look a fool doesn't bother you, does it? I suppose I deserve that." She had to take a deep breath and hold it for a moment to steady herself before she could go on, but there was no stopping now; painful as it might be, she could not simply walk away from this. "Why didn't you correct me when I said that you didn't have any ambition, and that you were really just a lazy bum without even a steady job?" Her voice almost cracked at the end, under the strain of repeating those stupid, silly charges. Then all the vibrancy died out of her tone, and she shook her head wearily. "Don't answer. I know. It didn't matter."

He drew the line back in, checked the lure and cast it again. "You didn't show any interest in what I might be doing." His voice was a little more gentle, but he didn't look at her. "You'd already made up your mind about me, and you didn't seem to want the facts to interfere. So I didn't bother you with them."

She chewed the tip of her little finger. It was certainly no more harsh a judgment than she deserved, she thought. But now that it was no longer true—was there any way to convince him of her change of heart? "I'm sorry," she said almost under her breath. "Of course I care, Penn."

It had a harsh ring of truth—too much truth, she realized abruptly, after it was too late to take it back. If he began to wonder just what she had meant—

She hurried on, almost stumbling over her words. "Why architecture, anyway? You started out to be a mechanical engineer." Would he even bother to answer? She doubted it.

Penn reeled his line in again, replaced the bait and cast it once more. Then he shrugged. "Architecture is the best part of engineering, with a whole lot of practical problem-solving mixed in. I hate dealing with nothing but abstractions."

She slowly released the breath that until then she hadn't known she was holding. "Is that why you build the houses yourself? Every board—every nail?"

"Do you really want to know?"

She nodded, her eyes fixed firmly on his face.

He was still staring out over the water. "Because I can point to it and say I did it all myself. I'm not just one cog in a machine."

Far out in the water something struck the lure, and Kaitlyn pulled her knees up and wrapped her arms around them and watched while he landed a big catfish.

"That's a beauty," he said. "Do you feel like catfish for dinner?"

And the subject of architecture and house-building was now closed, she thought. But at least it had been opened; for a couple of minutes there she had almost been able to peer inside him.

It would probably be better if she said no to the dinner invitation. There were Kathy's invitations to finish, and now that her conscience was clear and she could concentrate, the job wouldn't take long.

"I'd love catfish for dinner," she heard herself saying. "I've got the stuff for potato salad."

Penn smiled, and Kaitlyn felt a tiny little quiver that began in the pit of her stomach and radiated out till every cell was tingling.

You're a fool, she told herself. *You are most truly a fool, if you think there is any future in this. Nothing has changed.*

SHE KEPT TELLING HERSELF that for the next three days— long, lazy summer days. She felt as if she was trapped on a balance beam, forced to walk back and forth with no way to get off. Every time she caught a glimpse of Penn she felt as if she was doing a headstand; one false move, she knew, and she would crash. And it became more and more difficult to keep her balance as time went on, though not even the wishful longings of her own heart could convince her that there was anything serious about the time they spent together.

Penn was bored and restless, that was clear; while he waited for word on the Delaney property, he wanted something to do, and Kaitlyn was handy. So he invited her to swim with him, and skip rocks across the water in the twilight and walk up to the meadow to see the nest of baby rabbits that he'd discovered.

It was plain, however, that she was no more than idle entertainment. Though he seemed to enjoy her company, it was painfully clear to Kaitlyn that he didn't need it, for when she refused his invitations he simply went off alone. His cheerful whistle disappearing along the path would haunt her, reminding her that he didn't miss her much—if at all.

So she would sit over a pile of unaddressed envelopes and tell herself that there was no future in this sort of casual friendliness, that she'd do far better to cut things off right now.

But her heart rebelled at the idea of giving up all hope. Surely she was being too pessimistic, to think there was no future for them.

Not the kind of future I want, she thought. *Not the kind I need.*

But since she couldn't have what she wanted, anything was better than having nothing at all. And what was the big excitement about the future, anyway? The future was really only a hope, an ephemeral ideal—a tomorrow that might never come to be. Surely it would be far better to truly savor the joys that were possible today.

She grasped at the tiny gleam of comfort that philosophy offered. "And if I'm lucky," she whispered, "there might still be a succession of todays that I can store up to sustain me through a whole lot of empty tomorrows."

What was the alternative, after all? The only one she could see was to waste today, as well—and she had done that quite long enough.

She was not a girl with stardust in her eyes anymore, she reminded herself. She was a woman who had learned quite clearly the difference between reality and dreams. She was not going to get caught up in that confusion again.

So when Penn knocked at her door with a bucket in his hand and asked if she would like to come with him to the far end of the lake to see if the raspberries were ripe, she didn't hesitate for an instant.

It was breathlessly hot, and the boat's motion made a welcome breeze against her face and whipped her hair into tangles. The roar of the outboard motor made it impossible to talk, but she was almost grateful for that.

The raspberry patch was not only at the far end of the lake, but it lay on a hillside well above the water, in the softly filtered shade where the woods thinned gradually into meadowland. The bushes were thickly tangled and bristly, but the berries were plump and sweet and perfect, and Kaitlyn waded straight into the middle of a thicket, heedless of the thorns.

They ate more berries than they put in their buckets and finally sat down, replete, on a warm stretch of meadow grass. Kaitlyn hadn't felt this contented in years.

"You've got raspberry juice on your face," she accused him, and raised a finger to brush at Penn's chin.

"You can't get it off that way."

She smiled sweetly up at him. "Who said I was going to try to get it off? I was planning to rub it in and see what you look like when you're purple all over."

He seized her hands, but instead of the pull she expected, he gave her a gentle push; off balance, she sprawled on her back full-length on the grass. He was hovering over her an instant later, an elbow planted in the grass on each side of her, holding her hostage. "Then let's share the fun, shall we?" he suggested and brushed his chin against her cheek, her throat, her ear.

She shrieked resistance to the scratchy caress. "Didn't you bother to shave, Penn?"

"This morning. But I had no idea I was going to be doing this, or I wouldn't have."

"Well, stop it!"

"How do you ask nicely, Kitten?"

She fluttered here lashes at him. "Please, Penn—"

He pulled back for a second, and she saw the turbulent gray of his eyes. *I could drown myself in those eyes,* she thought.

The laughter died, and very slowly he lowered himself closer yet. There was no force in his touch, and yet there was a strength within him that was more frightening than violence would have been—and even more completely irresistible.

There was not even a hint of playfulness left by the time his lips met hers, just an insatiable hunger that seemed to reach down to her core and fill her heart with love for him. She gave a soft little sigh, knowing that she was practically melting against him, and not caring—

Then he pulled away, and Kaitlyn almost cried out; it was as if he had wrenched the very marrow from her bones as he tore himself from her.

Why? she wanted to scream. Why?

"Damn," he said, almost under his breath. "Where the hell did that blow in from?" He leaped up and stood with feet planted firmly, hands on hips, as he stared at the sky.

"What?" Kaitlyn said feebly. "I don't—"

Two huge cold raindrops hit her face, and one more drove through the thin cotton of her shirt like a knife blade against her overheated skin. She scrambled to her feet in shock. The sun was gone, and the western sky was suddenly full of tumbling clouds, huge masses of gray that seemed to be going all directions at once. The light of afternoon had faded to a pale gray dusk.

"I think we can make a run for it," Penn said. "There's lightning, but it's a long way off."

She was standing stock-still, staring at the clouds. "There wasn't supposed to be a storm!"

"So call the weather bureau and file a complaint." He grabbed the buckets and pulled her down the hill. "In the meantime, let's just head for the boat before it washes away and we have to walk, all right?"

The raindrops had been only the first isolated messengers—a nasty wake-up call from Mother Nature, Kaitlyn realized uneasily. The wind had come up, too, and the lake surface was becoming increasingly choppy as the minutes went by. Penn pushed the engine as close to full speed as he dared, racing the storm. Kaitlyn's stomach was threatening to desert her altogether by the time they reached the dock. Penn waved aside her offer of help with the boat and motor, and she decided there was no advantage in being a martyr, so she dashed for the cabin.

The rain came down with a sudden hiss, and by the time she reached her own door she was drenched. Her cotton shorts and shirt were plastered to her body, and her hair streamed rivulets down her face and neck. The wind sliced through her wet clothes like razor blades, and she shivered uncontrollably under the assault.

I might as well be naked in the middle of a blizzard, she thought. *I couldn't be any colder.*

She stumbled into the cabin, almost tripping over Schnoodle, and grabbed a pile of towels from the bathroom. But even a vigorous rubdown didn't help much; she was still shaking. So she knelt beside the fireplace and touched a match to the neatly built stack of kindling and logs.

She huddled beside it as the flame licked greedily at the dry wood and grew into comforting warmth. Was this what it would be like to spend the winter at Sapphire Lake? She found herself shivering again, not sure if it was in reaction to the drenching, or to the idea of being marooned up here. Had Penn thought it all out, she wondered. Had he truly considered the isolation, the difficulty of getting supplies, the loneliness of being the only person within miles....

Or perhaps, she thought, that's what he likes about the idea. Being entirely alone. It certainly doesn't seem to bother him—being able to depend only on himself....

Schnoodle's ears perked and he started to whine, just as the unmistakable sound of a fist hitting the door made Kaitlyn leap to her feet. It couldn't be Penn, could it? He wouldn't knock. Not unless he was afraid she might have walked in and stripped straight down to bare skin!

She flung the door open. "Don't just stand there in the rain getting—Marcus? What are you doing up here?"

He stepped across the threshold, holding a dripping umbrella. "I need to talk to you, Kaitlyn." He took in her drenched costume and towel-wrapped hair in one long glance. "What on earth have you been doing to yourself?"

"It wasn't an intentional shower, that's for sure." She was shivering again from the breeze. "I'm just drying off by the fire. Come in."

"Thank you; I will. I was playing golf this afternoon when a subject came up that I felt I should discuss with you."

Marcus took his trench coat off and draped it neatly across the back of a straight chair, and set his umbrella safely out of the range of sparks. He was playing golf, Kaitlyn thought in disbelief, but he was still prepared for a storm like this? There wasn't a wet spot on the man except at the cuffs of his neat golf slacks.

"—a great deal of talk," he was saying, "and I thought you should know what's being said."

"Said? About what?"

He looked a bit put out. "About you, Kaitlyn. And this Caldwell character. The entire town thinks you've moved up here to live with him."

That was no surprise, Kaitlyn thought; the big shock was that she hadn't anticipated the gossip herself. "The entire town?" She shook her head. "Oh, I think you must be wrong. It's probably not more than two-thirds. But thanks for the information, Marcus."

"Kaitlyn." Marcus's voice was grim. "You really must take this seriously."

"Why? Because you do?"

Marcus's lips set into a firm, thin line. "It doesn't help that you didn't see fit to tell me you were engaged to him once."

"I didn't tell you that because I wasn't," Kaitlyn said crisply. "And for your information, I'm not involved with him now, either. We're neighbors, that's all." Her conscience gave her a twinge, but she stilled it firmly. "For heaven's sake, Marcus, the man who lived next to

Mother's house on Belle Vista Avenue could have modeled for the fashion magazines, but I didn't notice you getting upset about him.''

"That," Marcus said sternly, "was different. I still care about you, Kaitlyn, and I don't like to see you make a public scandal of yourself like this."

The front door banged. "I'm not saying it's raining hard out there, but I saw a duck go by wearing a life jacket," Penn said. "Throw me a towel, would you, Kitten? Thanks—Oh, you've already built a fire, too." He mopped at his hair and dried his feet on the rug by the door, but didn't bother with the rest of him before crossing the room to the warmth of the blaze. "Hello, Wainwright."

He held out a large, wet hand; Marcus looked it over warily for telltale smears of oil and gasoline before half-heartedly extending his own.

Then Penn leaned over Kaitlyn, huddled on the brick hearth by the fire; she tried to send him a warning, but he seemed oblivious. She couldn't even duck away when his hand, still cold and wet, cupped her chin. He placed a long and leisurely kiss on her lips. "I left the berries on the porch," he said. "They've already been washed."

"Thanks," she said gloomily. "For nothing," she added under her breath.

Marcus stood up. "I see I've wasted my time," he said coldly as he reached for his raincoat.

"Oh, don't run off," Penn cajoled. "You must? Well, then, let me walk you out, at least. It's no trouble—I can't possibly get any wetter." He draped a companionable arm across Marcus's shoulders, and Kaitlyn heard him say just as the door banged behind them, "I understand you're to be congratulated for escaping a fate worse than death—"

Suddenly so furious that she couldn't bear it, Kaitlyn kicked the antique coal hod beside the fireplace. It was full of kindling and not as heavy as it looked. Still, her bare toes connected solidly with the iron, and she sat down abruptly, holding her foot between her hands and trying not to howl.

It would only make things worse if Penn came back in and found her sobbing. For it wasn't the ache in her foot she was crying about—and it wasn't because she was the subject of gossip back in Springhill, either.

"A fate worse than death"—those words drove home to her as never before that nothing was going to change. If he had felt the least bit serious about her, Penn wouldn't have said them. He obviously knew—and had known for some time—about her broken engagement. But he'd never even mentioned it, and he certainly would have if he had any desire for a long-term relationship. Congratulating Marcus on escaping...

She ought to have kicked Penn instead of the coal hod. Or perhaps she should have kicked herself.

For no matter how sensible she'd told herself she was being, still she had hoped that someday things would be different—and now those hopes had been crushed once more, with cruel finality.

"Well, that takes care of him," Penn said, cheerfully. "The fire was a lovely idea, Kitten. Let's—"

Kaitlyn wheeled on him. "Did you have to do that?"

His eyebrows lifted slightly. "Did you really want him to stay to dinner?"

"For all you know, I did!"

"Really?" He sounded perfectly pleasant. He crossed the room and picked up his towel again. "I thought it was safe to assume that when a woman tosses an engagement ring into an ashtray she doesn't want the man in question hanging around anymore."

She bit her lip. Hard. So he not only knew the fact of her broken engagement; he knew the details, too. "And what would you know about the rules concerning engagement rings?" she said coldly.

There was a flicker, behind his eyes. "Not much, I admit. Nevertheless, I didn't exactly want him hanging around, either."

"Oh?" Kaitlyn's voice was dangerously quiet. "Well, if that isn't just like you, Penn. A dog in the manger. You didn't want me ten years ago, and you don't want me now. You just want to cause trouble!"

He stopped massaging himself with the towel and said, very smoothly, "Did I say I didn't want you?" He tossed the towel aside and took a step closer to her. "Foolish me."

Suddenly he seemed very big—not threatening, exactly, but overwhelming. There was no place to go to avoid him; he seemed to be blocking her path.

"And foolish you," he went on, softly. "After that roll in the raspberry bushes this afternoon, how could you doubt it? It was you who started it, if you remember—or do you need a reminder?"

"I don't need anything from you." Her voice was low and hoarse. She had to clear her throat, but she managed to say it. "Get out, Penn. Don't bother me again."

He stopped dead, less than arm's length from her. "Kaitlyn," he said.

She turned her back on him. She was hugging her arms across her chest as tightly as she could, trying to stop herself from shaking. It seemed to be forever that they stood there, silent. Outside the world was coming apart at the seams, but in the cabin the only sound was the hiss of the fire.

"I'll talk to Marcus tomorrow, and set him straight," Penn said quietly. A moment later the door closed softly behind him.

I'm glad that's what he thinks, she told herself fiercely. It was a whole lot better than the truth.

From the corner of her eye she saw the flash of lightning, and a split second later thunder crashed and rolled around her. The cabin seemed to shake under the weight of the sound. She turned toward the window, knowing she was too late to see, but at that instant the sky seemed to light once more with the radiance of a million flashbulbs. For one split second it was supernaturally brilliant, bright enough to see across the lake. She could see the shoreline, where the turbulent waves pounded against the sand. She could see the roiling clouds above, going in a hundred different directions. She could see the huge old mulberry tree beside the Caldwell cabin as it bent and split and twisted and began to fall—

And as that eerie light died away, the last thing she saw was the dark figure of a man silhouetted against the tree— pathetically small against its massive bulk, and directly in its path.

CHAPTER TEN

SHE WAS OUT the door before she even realized she had moved, and she ran through the mud and muck, scarcely feeling the cold splash of rain on her face or the sharpness of gravel against the bare soles of her feet.

She was screaming as she ran. Not his name, or any words at all, but long pure shrieks of animal anguish, already seeing in her mind the inevitable. Penn, sprawled under that huge mulberry, helpless. Injured. Dead—

The earth seemed to still be shaking from the impact of the enormous trunk, and the air was filled with the nauseating sulfurous smell of hot ozone. The sound of the crash was still echoing across the valley—or was it merely the thunder that she heard?

The irregular flicker of lightning showed her the damage in surreal fragments, as if she was watching some frayed old motion picture.

The tree had split down the center and half of it now lay against the side of the Caldwell cabin. One wall of the sleeping porch had been caved in, and a good part of the deck was shattered. The other half of the tree had fallen outward, across the driveway and the winding road. A branch as big around as Kaitlyn's waist had bounced off the top of the old pickup truck, and she closed her eyes tightly for a moment to try to blot out the image of what that kind of blow would do to a human body. She didn't want to see.

But if there was any help for him at all, it would have to come from her. So she gulped and forced herself to look, to feel her way around the tree and try to peer under the debris.

In the darkness, she tripped over a torn-up root and went down hard into a puddle. Only then, as she choked on the muddy water, did she realize that she was still trying to scream.

In the sudden silence, she heard Penn's voice calling her name. It was faint and far away—or was that the storm, playing tricks with the air and the echoes? She raised her head and tried to answer, and something plucked her out of the water, lifting her back to her feet as lightly as a feather. She fought, trying to break free so she could go to him— "Kaitlyn, dammit, stop!" he ordered, gasping. "I'll sock you in the jaw if I have to."

She went limp in his arms, sagging against him, her hands clawing at his wet shirt. "I saw you," she almost babbled. "I thought it must have fallen on you."

"I suppose you were coming to make sure?"

"How can you say such a thing?" she screamed at him between her sobs. And then she realized that he couldn't be badly injured if he was standing there, instead of lying helpless under the tree. And not only standing, but supporting her weight as well as his own. Nothing else mattered to her then, as long as he was all right.

Her strength came flooding back and she flung her arms around him, squeezing as hard as she could, trying with all her might to keep him safe. She was numb with cold except where her body met his—breasts and hips and thighs and arms and mouth.

"I hate to break up the party." Penn's voice was breathless. "But lightning *does* strike twice, and there's still a storm going on."

She couldn't bring herself to let go of him, and so they walked rather awkwardly back to the A-frame, with her arms clutched around his waist.

Something thumped against the door just as they reached it. It was Schnoodle, Kaitlyn realized, flinging his body against it, trying to push his way out to come after her. Thank heavens he hadn't managed to get out, she thought; he'd have been lost forever in the storm.

The dog's anguished howl broke off in midnote as soon as he saw them, and his feet scrambled for traction against the hard floor as he followed them to the fireplace.

Penn knelt to rebuild the fire, and Kaitlyn sagged down onto the stone hearth, hardly aware of the muddy water dripping from her hair, her clothes, her chin—or even the dog, who was single-mindedly wiping his tongue across every square inch of human skin within his reach.

There was a trickle of blood on Penn's forehead, she saw, and a streak on his arm. "You're hurt," she said dully.

He shook his head. "Nothing serious. A few of the small branches lashed me on the way down, that's all."

She thought bemusedly, the tree misses him by inches, and he says, "that's all?" She started to shake a little.

"A bit close for comfort, but haven't you heard about my guardian angel? He's had more difficult jobs."

"I wish you wouldn't joke about it." Her voice was trembling, too.

He put another log on the fire and sat back on his heels to look at her thoughtfully. "I'm sorry, Kitten. Does it really matter?"

"Of course it doesn't matter," she said furiously. "I'd have run out there to help a squirrel who was trapped, or a rat, or..."

Her whole body was quivering now. He moved quickly to the hearth and put his arms around her. "Time for a little hysterics treatment, I think," he mused.

She tried to shake him off, but she was fighting her own longings as well as his strength, and it was only a few seconds before she sagged helplessly in his arms. It was warm there, with her back to the fire. The tenseness in her muscles gradually seeped away.

"Better?" he asked.

She wanted to deny it and to stay there beside him forever—or as close to forever as she could manage.

"Then off with you to have a shower. We're both soaked—we're going to have pneumonia if we don't get warm and dry." He pulled her to her feet. "And clean wouldn't hurt, either, in your case."

The gentle attempt at humor only made her want to cry. She shook her head a little to try to clear the tears away, but the motion set them free instead, and two hot drops rolled down her cheeks.

Penn cupped her chin in his hand and turned her face up to his, and caught her tears with the tip of his tongue. The butterfly-light touch against her cheek sent a wave of shockingly strong sensation flickering through her, and she moaned softly and leaned against him—not with the intention of being seductive, but because her knees had suddenly turned to sand.

He said something gruff under his breath and pulled her suddenly close, and his mouth came down on hers without a hint of gentleness.

As if he was being driven past the point of reason, Kaitlyn thought, just as she had been for days now. That was only fair; she had long ago lost all common sense—

But the horrid little demon of memory poked an uncomfortable pin into her. *Past the point of reason, lacking all common sense—*

Once he had accused her of manipulating him into making love to her, in the hope of trapping him forever. Was the past to repeat itself now?

She tried to stamp out the notion, but then her fingers bushed across his face, and the sticky blood that still oozed from the wound on his forehead brought her back to reality. She let her hands drop to his chest, held herself a fraction of an inch away from him as casually as she could, and said, "That scratch needs to be cleaned."

Penn gently touched the tip of her nose. "I'll have a shower as soon as you're finished, and then you can work on it."

There was no point in discussing the matter; she could be clean and dry—and so could he—long before she could argue him into giving up the notion that ladies went first. So she climbed the stairs to the bathroom and turned the shower on full force.

At least the time spent sitting by the fire meant that she wasn't actually dripping anymore, but the mud that had started to dry on her arms and legs was making her skin itch unbearably. Meanwhile, her clothes were still unpleasantly soggy. She practically had to roll her blouse off; the mud had almost glued it to her skin. Her face was freckled with splotches of grime—no wonder Penn had said that being clean would improve her immensely!

When she came back downstairs, wrapped in a big terrycloth robe and still rubbing her hair with a towel, she was greeted with the heavenly smell of hot chocolate. Penn handed her a mug.

"I was thinking," she said hesitantly. "The wall of your cabin—it was all smashed in."

Penn nodded. "The sleeping porch got a good jolt."

"Everything inside is going to be ruined, isn't it?"

He shrugged. "It can't be helped. I don't have anything to close the hole up with, even if I was willing to climb around out there and tempt the lightning again. The worst is over; the rain is starting to lighten up now."

She glanced at the clock, and was surprised to see that it was barely time for sunset. The darkness made it seem almost the middle of the night.

Penn carried his mug upstairs with him and Kaitlyn went back to the fire. He'd added another log, and she pulled a woolly blanket out of the steamer trunk that served as a coffee table and spread it out directly in front of the flames so she could toast her toes more comfortably. Her feet were starting to hurt from running over the gravel.

"Not bright, Kaitlyn," she told herself. "It's certainly no credit to you that he's walking around! You dash out to save him from the lightning, and you end up falling in a puddle and having to be rescued yourself."

But it certainly showed how out of control she'd become. She hadn't forgotten the sound of her screams—and she wouldn't be able to, she reflected dryly, until her abused throat had a chance to heal.

Schnoodle flopped down beside her to bask in the warmth, and Kaitlyn caressed his soft coat as she stared into the flames and studied her soul.

There could be no more games with herself, she thought. No more pretending that she could easily do without him. No more imagining that it didn't really matter. She loved Penn as deeply as it was possible to love, and so there was only one choice left for her to make. She would take whatever she could have—whatever part of him he was willing to share with her.

And what if he isn't willing to do that? she asked herself. *What if he thinks I'm manipulating him once more?*

But surely there was a way to make him understand that she had learned something from all this, and that she could accept whatever it was he was willing to give, and be contented with it—

Can you, Kaitlyn? The whisper of conscience nagged at her. *Can you honestly promise him that?*

But there was no other way. This road would certainly be a painful one. When he walked away—

Because sooner or later, he inevitably would. She'd already recognized the restlessness in him. It might be postponed, but it couldn't be denied.

She squared her shoulders. When he went, she would deal with it, that was all. It would hurt, but certainly no more than if she tried to turn away from him now. To lose him would be awful, but to deliberately do without him would be like choosing to die altogether—a premature death. Surely it was better to have something than nothing—

The power flickered once, twice and went off. With no other light in the room, the fire cast weird and wonderful shadows. By the time Kaitlyn had found a candle and managed to stand it upright by dripping a pool of wax onto a saucer, Penn had finished his shower.

She heard him feeling his way across the shadowed loft to the spiral stairs. She looked up almost fearfully to see him standing there, leaning against the wrought-iron railing and looking down at her, and she turned quickly back to stare at the candle. She heard his steps descending, then crossing the hardwood floor, but she didn't look up again till he dropped to the blanket beside her. Then, a little surprised that he had come to her there, she couldn't help darting a glance at him.

He was wrapped in a garish tartan bathrobe. "Good thing someone was careless enough to leave his robe behind," he mused and reached out to poke at the fire.

"No guest of mine," she snapped. "It's been hanging on the back of the bathroom door ever since I moved in."

She was annoyed when he smiled.

"I wasn't asking, Kitten. I didn't need to." He put the poker down and slid his arm around her. A moment later, Kaitlyn found herself lying full-length on the blanket, with no clear notion of how she had gotten there—just that it was very smooth, and that it had involved no effort of hers.

"Now—" he whispered against her lips. "Are you really sorry we waited till we were clean?" His mouth moved softly to the point of her chin and along the line of her jaw to her tiny earlobe. "Not that I have a fetish about soap and water, you understand, and not that I didn't find you just as attractive this afternoon out in the berries when you were warm and covered with sticky juice—but I do draw the line when I find myself kissing mud instead of skin."

And then his voice trailed off as he suited action to words, taking her lips with an urgency that sent long shudders of pleasure rippling through her.

He knows, she thought. *He understands what I've been trying to tell him. That it's all right, really, whatever happens—*

. She moaned a little and tried to pull him down to her, and he caught her hands and held them gently, and began to caress her, very softly, with his mouth. He nibbled at the delicate skin of her throat, then found his way slowly to the hollow between her breasts, and ever so gently teased the terry cloth aside. . . .

On that night long ago when they had first made love, she had been an inexperienced girl, eager to please him; her own pleasure had been an afterthought. Now, he showed her that she was still inexperienced, woman though she was—and he taught her things about her own capacity for pleasure that she had never dreamed. And this time when they joined together it was with a stunning sense of fulfillment, and of joy so powerful that it made her ache and want to weep.

A little later he sat up, reached for a small log and then sat there with it in his hand, silently watching the fire.

Kaitlyn lay quietly and studied him through almost-closed eyelashes as the firelight played against the angles of his face. The silence drew out, interrupted only by the snapping of the flames, until it was almost painful. She thought of a dozen ways to break it, but the sentences chased each other through her mind until nothing sounded casual or sincere.

Still, she couldn't stand the silence anymore. Better to have it gone, even if what she said sounded arch or coy or stupid. "You must be thinking heavy thoughts," she murmured. Not bad, she thought. Her voice was light, easy, casual—it was obvious that she didn't want to press for an answer.

"Very heavy."

He sounded almost somber, and the unexpected seriousness made her draw a sharp, concerned, frightened breath.

Not now, she wanted to plead. *Can't you at least let me have a little joy, just a tiny space of time in which I can dream?*

But if she said anything of the sort, it would bring on the inevitable—the explanations, the warnings, the somber discussions—the very things she wanted to avoid. Instead, she sat up and pulled the blanket around her shoulders and said, as lightly as she could, "I don't know about you, but I don't think a bucket of raspberries is a balanced meal. I'm starving."

He turned to look at her, then, with a smile that didn't quite light his eyes.

He's afraid, she thought. Afraid of what she would want—perhaps even demand. It made her feel sad that it had happened so quickly, but she knew it had been inevitable; it was impossible to live entirely in that land of magic, where a touch conveyed a thought, and two minds were as one. She jumped up to rummage through her kitchen, mostly so he couldn't see the moisture that sparkled in her eyes.

They made an adventure of dinner, heating a can of beef stew in a cast-iron skillet, and toasting bread on long forks over the flames. It took all the strength she had to treat him casually, to keep her voice playful and the subject light.

"It's like being a pioneer crossing the plains in a covered wagon," Kaitlyn reflected as she mopped up the last of her stew with a piece of bread. "I wonder if they ate so much."

"Only if they were lucky."

She opened a bag of marshmallows and impaled one on her fork. "Too bad we don't have chocolate bars and graham crackers," she murmured. The marshmallow turned golden over the embers, and she savored its soft sweetness.

"Some pioneer you'd make," Penn snorted. "You want all the comforts." The light in his eyes made her duck her head and reach for two more marshmallows, not quite certain if it was desire for him or the threat of tears that made her feel so uneasy inside.

"Will you show me your houses sometime?" she asked suddenly.

Penn's eyes darkened and his brows drew together.

Kaitlyn wondered why; surely there was nothing so very threatening about showing her his drawings. Then she remembered the storm, and her eyes widened with fear. "Your drawings—the rain...?"

Penn shook his head. "Unless the sleeping porch actually tore away from the main part of the house—which I don't think it did—the inner rooms should still be dry. I'll know in the morning."

There was nothing that could be done before then, she knew. There could be no assessment of the structural damage till it was light.

Her marshmallows were done; she absentmindedly tried to eat them both at the same time, and ended up with goo all over her face. Penn watched for a moment as she tried to clean it off, then helpfully began to remove it himself, half-licking and half-kissing.

And by the time he was finished with that, and had doused the fire and led her upstairs, Kaitlyn no longer remembered that he hadn't ever answered her question.

SUNLIGHT POURING through the balcony windows woke her the next morning—brilliant sunlight, cascading down from a crisp, clear, bright blue sky—and she peered out at the world that looked as fresh and newly washed as if it had just come from the laundry. Then she realized that Penn was nowhere to be seen.

His absence didn't bother her at first; it was later than she'd thought, and no doubt he was already inspecting the damage the fallen tree had done.

But she found no sign of him downstairs, and no evidence that he had been there. The electrical power had come back on sometime during the night, but he hadn't even made coffee. She told herself it was nothing; he would have been anxious to check the cabin. But when she went out to see the damage for herself, only the birds greeted her.

The hole in the side of the cabin was a gaping wound. Kaitlyn stared at it, aghast, wondering if Penn had taken one look and decided it wasn't worth the work of repairing. Or had everything that had happened—the storm, the damage to truck and cabin, the explosive evening with Kaitlyn herself—made him conclude that it was time to move on?

Her common sense told her such a thing was unlikely. His car was still there—blocked by the fallen tree, she reminded herself.

But the little nugget of fear settled at the bottom of her stomach. It was the harsh truth that he had left her once, and she knew that sooner or later it would happen again. She had made her choices with that knowledge firmly in mind, but the facts didn't make things easier.

Then she heard a whistle, and Schnoodle's cheerful yapping. Penn was coming down the path, a chain saw cradled in his arms. "I borrowed it from the guy a couple of houses down," he explained. "We aren't going anywhere as long as that tree is blocking the road."

She tried to play it casual. "What's so important about getting out, anyway?" she said with a shrug.

He grinned and kissed her lightly. "Don't you remember? I told you I'd have a talk with Marcus today."

Something snapped deep inside her. "That's right," she agreed woodenly. "To set him straight, and tell him that I don't mean a damned thing to you and I never did—"

She saw the shock in his face, so like that night ten years ago when she'd implied a future that he didn't want.

You asked for this, Kaitlyn, she told herself coldly.

She'd always known that there would be no promises from Penn—at least not the kind she wanted. She had told herself she could live without promises, but whether that was actually true or not made no difference now. Whatever she said, it would look as if she was making demands, and that alone would be enough to drive him away. She had set herself up for this; it was no one's fault but her own. There was nothing she could say now that would make it better.

So she turned on her heel and stalked back into the cabin.

"Dammit, Kaitlyn!" The door slammed as he followed her in. "I'm heartily sick of this!"

And nothing you say can possibly make it worse, either, she thought. *So why not stop bottling it up inside?*

"You're sick of it?" she shouted. "I don't know what the hell you're thinking of, Penn Caldwell! Yourself, that's obvious. Well, you don't have to tell me again what you think of me—I still remember it from last time."

He winced at that.

But she quickly found there was no satisfaction in wounding him. All the anger died away in an instant, and left her feeling limp and hopeless. "Just go ahead and leave," she whispered. "That's what you'll do, sooner or later—" She turned aside with a helpless gesture.

"I'm not going anywhere, Kaitlyn." It was very quiet, very firm. "Not for a long time."

She didn't bother to answer. What was *a long time,* anyway? Time was relative.

"I've got the Delaney property," he said. "They agreed to the terms yesterday."

It should have been a breath of reprieve. She should have instantly started to figure out how many months it would take to build a house—how long she could have him, provided that she didn't make the mistake of growing overpossessive and lose him through her own folly. But she didn't.

"That's nice," she said flatly. "But all of a sudden it doesn't seem to matter anymore. It won't work, Penn. I want promises—and you can't give them."

He would leave now, she thought. He would probably be so anxious to escape that he'd go straight through the wall....

Instead, he said very calmly, "What sort of promises, Kaitlyn?"

She stared at him and realized that her hearing had suddenly gone bizarre. She'd have to have it checked, she thought, and shook her head, trying to clear it.

He came across the room and seized her by the shoulders. "Answer me," he said fiercely. "For once, would you open up those glorious green eyes of yours and look at the way things really are instead of what you think they must be?"

She blinked up at him in wonder.

"Why the hell do you imagine I want that particular piece of ground, anyway? I can build houses anywhere—and I have. I didn't have to choose Springhill."

"I don't know." It was little more than a whisper, almost shaken out of her.

The handsomeness had drained out of his face, leaving only harsh lines and angles. "Because as soon as I saw you again, I knew what had been missing in my life for the past ten years."

She was too stunned to move, and she couldn't remember how to breathe. If it hadn't been for his hands still clutching her shoulders she would probably have collapsed.

"I came home for Angela's wedding," he said. "I don't know why. Call it a sudden attack of nostalgia. Coming at a time when I was at loose ends, it sounded like a reasonable thing to do. But that day in the church when I saw you again, I knew you weren't just a girl I used to care about. You were—''

He let her go, and she found herself leaning against the back of the couch, grateful for its solid strength. ''You could have said something,'' she muttered.

''No—I couldn't. Don't you see, Kaitlyn? You wouldn't have trusted me, no matter what I said. I used you ten years ago. I didn't mean to, I swear I never intended what happened—but that doesn't change what I did. I walked out on you, as cruelly as any man ever did. I destroyed the trust you had put in me.''

This was no slick and facile apology, she knew, but hard edged, unpleasant truth, and obviously it had long ago been considered and admitted. Kaitlyn put her hands to her face; her cheeks were burning.

''I knew I would have to be patient in order to rebuild that trust—because I couldn't take advantage of you again. I knew that you wouldn't believe whatever I said, but I thought that sooner or later you'd realize that I was around to stay. That's why I wanted the Delaney property—to give me something to do while I waited. I figured by the time I built half a dozen houses on that tract of land—''

''Half a dozen?'' The words were little more than a croak.

''—you'd get the message. But last night, I thought—'' He gave a long, tired sigh, and admitted, ''I didn't want to think last night, that's the real truth. I didn't want to wait any longer, to be patient another day—so I told myself that it was all right, that you understood I was different now. Obviously you cared about me, the way you came tearing out into that storm—and this was your way of telling me that you had forgiven what I'd done.''

"All I understood was that I wanted you," she whispered. "I didn't want to look at what would happen after that."

He sounded discouraged, and angry. "And so we ripped open old wounds, and now we have to let them heal all over again."

He started to turn away.

She pushed herself awkwardly from the couch, and caught at his arm. When he turned to her, she raised her fingertips to his forehead and stroked the small scratch made by the tree branch. "Perhaps those wounds never would have healed, left to themselves, hidden away like that," she said. "But now we have another chance. If we share them—talk about them..."

Slowly, his arms closed around her, and she gave him a tremulous smile and then buried her face in his neck and tried not to shed the tears that burned her eyes.

He held her quietly for a long time, his face pressed against her hair. When he began to talk, his voice was so soft that she almost couldn't catch the words.

"When you're twenty years old, it isn't very fashionable to actually like your parents," he said. "And I don't mean to say we never had disagreements. But I didn't just lose my parents in that boating accident, Kitten. I lost my two best friends, as well. I can tell you all the psychological jargon about survivor's guilt, because I made it and they didn't. And there was regular guilt, too, because I thought I should have been able to turn that wheel and get out of the way."

"But that wasn't possible," she whispered. "Nobody could have avoided that accident."

"Guilt isn't logical, Kitten. And I had lots of things to feel guilty about, like the fight I'd been having with my father over whether I should drop out of college for a while, till I figured out what I wanted to do. When, suddenly, I was free to do it, I felt as if I'd killed him.''

A tiny spark of relief sprang to life in Kaitlyn's heart. She'd always blamed herself because he'd dropped out of school. But it hadn't been her fault, after all.

''For a month after the accident, I was either too numb to know what was going on, or I hurt like hell every minute of the day. And when I could comprehend anything at all, I told myself that the answer was never to care about anyone so much again. Then they couldn't hurt me, and I couldn't hurt them. It was perfectly simple.''

She hugged him as tightly as she could, wishing she'd understood any of this, back then. Her own innocent simplicity—pretending that it would all go away if she ignored it long enough—made her feel just a little sick.

''But you were there, and I couldn't push you away. For one thing, you wouldn't be pushed. And then came that awful night when I needed your warmth and your sanity and your beauty—and it was only afterward, when you held me—''

''What did I say?'' she whispered. ''I don't remember, Penn. I swear, I don't remember.''

He raised his head and looked down at her. '' 'Nothing can come between us now,' '' he quoted dryly

''Oh, Penn.''

''That's when I realized that I was doing it all over again, despite my best intentions—loving you, and leaving myself open to that awful hurt. Fearing—because if losing parents was so awful, what would it be like to lose a lover? Or a child?''

Her tears brimmed, and she tried futilely to blink them away. ''Then it wasn't—''

''It wasn't you, darling. It was me, and the fear that I would lose anyone I let myself care about—and the knowledge that if it was through my fault, it would finish me.'' He released a long, painful breath. "And so I deliberately cast aside the most beautiful thing that was left in my life—and I ran."

She hugged him closer still, and tried to tell him with her touch—because there were no words—how this agonizing honesty was affecting her.

"I'm not sorry about leaving," he added, with what was almost defiance. "If I had stayed, I would have resented it."

She nodded. "And me." It was not pleasant to acknowledge that, but there was peace in knowing the truth.

"For a while, I convinced myself that nothing mattered but today. Why bother? Why get involved? It will all be wiped out tomorrow. Eventually I got over that, and for the past few years I've at least been making a contribution to the world, instead of asking nothing and giving nothing. But it wasn't until that day at St. Matthew's when I saw you again that I knew there was still unfinished business here. Kaitlyn, if you will only take me back, and let me show you what you mean to me—'' He was whispering against her hair. "I'll never hurt you again."

"Yes, you will, Penn," she said unsteadily. "And I'll no doubt hurt you, too—because loving sometimes hurts. But never again will we hide the pain and pretend that it doesn't matter. That's the difference."

He took it for the answer it was, and kissed her long and softly as if he would never let her go.

"You've been so restless," she murmured. "I was afraid. I thought you were getting anxious to be gone."

He shook his head. "No. Just to know. To have this settled."

"But you didn't say anything when I broke my engagement," she protested. "So I thought it didn't matter to you what I did, and it almost broke my heart when you congratulated Marcus on getting out of marrying me—''

"But of course," Penn said. He held her a few inches away from him. The old sparkle had sprung back into his eyes and his voice. "Marrying you *would* have been a fate worse than death."

"Dammit, Penn," she objected, and stopped dead. The one thing he hadn't mentioned—hadn't offered her—was marriage.

It's all right, she told herself stoutly. *I am sure, now, that he loves me, and that's the only thing that matters.*

"For Marcus," he added smoothly. "You see, Kitten, I never did believe in your engagement. If you had been serious about Marcus, you'd have married him long ago—or slept with him at least. But if you were willing to wait eight months—''

He saw the uncertainty in her eyes, and caught her close again. "Kitten, darling, I'm sorry. I was convinced you'd never marry Marcus, but I can't say that was much comfort, because I wasn't so sure you'd ever marry me, either. Will you?"

She choked on the lump in her throat, and he had to pat her on the back for almost a minute before she could stop coughing and breathe properly again.

"That's not flattering," he complained.

"Yes," she whispered. "Yes, I'll marry you."

There was a light in his eyes that made her think that she'd glimpsed heaven—but he wouldn't have been Penn if he'd said something sentimental. "Too bad we didn't get this all sorted out last week," he mused. "We could have just taken over Laura's arrangements—church and guests and cake and all."

"We couldn't have gotten a license in time."

"Want to bet?"

Something clicked in her head. "You were coming out of the courthouse the other day."

He grinned. "And I wasn't applying for building permits. But in any case, it doesn't matter—we'll have all kinds of time to get a license."

That made her frown because it didn't sound right, somehow. "We will?"

"Of course. You'll want the whole show, right? I warn you, however; I am not Marcus, and I am not willing to wait forever. If you want a splashy wedding, fine—we'll have it. But in the meantime I'll be doing my absolute best to persuade you to live with me."

"Where?" she asked, remembering the caved-in wall.

"I'll build us a house. Now stop distracting me when I'm trying to warn you about my methods. I don't play fair, you know. Shall I demonstrate?"

He didn't wait for an answer, and by the time he allowed Kaitlyn to come up for air, she was dizzy.

"I don't think we'll wait for a big wedding," she managed.

Penn looked concerned. "That's the point. We're not waiting for the wedding, no matter what size it is. But your clients wouldn't understand if you didn't have a major splash."

"The ones who know you certainly will!" She remembered what he had said about Sabrina's elaborate plans, and snuggled against him. "Penn, you were right. It's the marriage that counts—not the ceremony. I don't want to get so caught up in the details that I can't have fun at my own wedding."

"We'll talk about it later," he promised, and she nodded.

But she didn't think she would change her mind. It would be a new challenge, she thought, to create a nice wedding that didn't take forever to plan, or cost the earth, or cause that last-minute war of nerves that she had come to think was inevitable. A lot of her clients might like that idea, too. . . .

But there would be time to think about that later; there were more important considerations at the moment, like telling him with every cell of her body and with every whisper of sensation how much she loved him.

She obviously succeeded, for a few minutes later Penn said breathlessly, "You were right, Kitten. We'll just let the damned tree lie there. I wonder why I thought it was so important to get out of here in the next week or two, anyway?"

EPILOGUE

"JUST ONE MORE," Jill said, "and then we'll let Audrey go while we finish up the shots of the bridesmaids. Kaitlyn's veil isn't flowing quite right on that side, Audrey. Can you fix it?"

Audrey fussed with the drifting chiffon. Her hands were shaking a little. A standard case of mother-of-the-bride nerves, Kaitlyn thought. Or was it more than that? Audrey's lower lip was trembling a little, too. . . .

Jill's photo flash popped. "Perfect," she said with satisfaction. "Now if we can get all of the bridesmaids together—"

But Kaitlyn wasn't listening. "What is it, Mother?"

Audrey tried to smile, but tears gleamed in her eyes. "I wasn't going to tell you. It's so silly. But I just remembered your christening bonnet. Oh, Kaitlyn, how could I have forgotten it, on this special day?"

Christening bonnet? For an instant Kaitlyn thought her mother had gone around the bend. Then she remembered the delicate bit of linen and lace. It had started out as the handkerchief Audrey had carried on her wedding day, and when Kaitlyn was born, a few deft stitches and a bit of ribbon had made it into a bonnet. Now, on her wedding day, Kaitlyn was supposed to clip the stitches and have a handkerchief again, until the next generation came along.

"It was the special 'something old' I wanted you to carry," Audrey said. Her voice cracked. "I put it aside as I was unpacking, and then I forgot it."

Kaitlyn hugged her gently. "I have something old," she reminded. "Your dress." She brushed the delicate ivory satin sleeve of the gown she wore. "Don't be superstitious, Mother. Besides, tears are far worse for the bride than a forgotten handkerchief is."

Audrey smiled bravely. "I know, dear. Nothing is going to keep this marriage from working, is it? You and Penn—" She kissed Kaitlyn gently. "I'm so glad, darling."

Kaitlyn watched her leave the little anteroom at the back of St. Matthew's. For an instant, she felt like crying herself. Superstition or not, that handkerchief was important to her. It had been her father's gift to his fiancée, the last before Audrey became his bride. And since he wasn't here today to walk Kaitlyn down the aisle...

But there was no time for regrets, so she joined the group of young women in snappy dark green cocktail dresses and laughed with them as Stephanie muttered, "Bridesmaids? With almost a dozen kids among us, we're hardly any kind of maids."

The carillon chimed the hour just as Jill took the last shot, of an excited flower girl with her basket of blossoms, and the little troop moved out into the entryway.

The final notes of a haunting violin melody floated through the air, and the church settled into the expectant hush that was so familiar to Kaitlyn. The last guests were in place; her mother had been seated.

"I guess it's time," Kaitlyn said. Her voice quavered a little.

Footsteps pounded up the staircase from the lower level of the church, and an usher burst into sight. "Don't," he gasped. "Don't give the cue yet. We can't find Penn."

Kaitlyn could actually feel the blood draining from her face. "Has he been here at all?"

Another usher appeared on the steps. "Yeah, he was here."

He can't possibly stand me up at the church, Kaitlyn thought. "He didn't happen to mention Botswana or the Sahara Desert or Tahiti, did he?" she asked.

"He didn't say anything." The usher shrugged. "He was just gone all of a sudden."

A third usher peered hopefully up the steps. "Is he back here?"

Kaitlyn put her hands to her head. "I am never going to go through this again," she muttered.

"I should hope not." The calm voice came from behind her, near the doors that opened to the street. "One to a customer, that's always been my understanding."

Kaitlyn wheeled round. Relief flooded through her as she saw Penn standing in the doorway, tall and elegant and perfectly at ease in his black tuxedo. Only his wind-ruffled hair hinted that everything was not as it should be.

He looked around at the crowd. "Nice of you all to form this reception committee. Why are we short one usher, Kaitlyn?"

"Where have you *been*, Penn Caldwell?"

His fingers brushed the veil at her temple, and his voice softened to an intimate murmur. "I'm sorry I'm late, Kitten." He pulled a delicate scrap of fabric from his pocket.

Kaitlyn's fingers trembled as she took the christening bonnet from his hand. "Mother sent you across town for this?"

"No. In fact, she doesn't know I went after it. But when she told me—I thought you'd want to have it."

Kaitlyn's eyes blurred a little. She nodded.

"It would be a shame to break the tradition, don't you think?" he whispered. "Someday, when we bring a child here to be christened . . . Ah, here's our missing usher. I thought you'd be along sooner or later." He kissed the tip of Kaitlyn's nose. "Meet me at the front of the church in two minutes, Kitten?"

Kaitlyn nodded. "Can I trust you not to get sidetracked between here and there?"

He didn't answer, but he flashed a thumbs-up sign at her as he led a parade of ushers down the steps, on their way to the altar.

And as the first soft strains of the wedding march drifted through the church, Kaitlyn fingered the delicate linen and lace of the bonnet, and smiled.

HARLEQUIN
Romance®

WELCOME TO

The quintessential small town, where everyone
knows everybody else!

Finally, books that capture the pleasure of tuning in to your favorite
TV show!

GREAT READING...GREAT SAVINGS...AND A FABULOUS FREE
GIFT!

Each book set in Tyler is a self-contained love story; together, the
twelve novels stitch the fabric of the community. The covers honor the
old American tradition of quilting; each cover depicts a patch of the
large Tyler quilt.

With Tyler you can receive a fabulous gift, ABSOLUTELY FREE, by
collecting proofs-of-purchase found in each Tyler book. And use our
special Tyler coupons to save on your next TYLER book purchase.

Join your friends at Tyler for the seventh book, ARROWPOINT by
Suzanne Ellison,
available in September.

*Rumors fly about the death at the old lodge! What happens when
Renata Meyer finds an ancient Indian sitting cross-legged on her lawn?*

If you missed *Whirlwind* (March), *Bright Hopes* (April), *Wisconsin Wedding* (May), *Monkey
Wrench* (June), *Blazing Star* (July) or *Sunshine* (August) and would like to order them, send
your name, address, zip or postal code, along with a check or money order for $3.99 for each
book ordered (please do not send cash), plus 75¢ postage and handling ($1.00 in Canada),
payable to Harlequin Reader Service, to:

In the U.S.

3010 Walden Avenue
P.O. Box 1325
Buffalo, NY 14269-1325

In Canada

P.O. Box 609
Fort Erie, Ontario
L2A 5X3

Please specify book title(s) with your order.
Canadian residents add applicable federal and provincial taxes.

TYLER-7